About the Author

Sophie Peacock lives in Ely, Cambridgeshire with her family and animals.

Zari Kingston

Sophie Peacock

Zari Kingston

Olympia Publishers
London

www.olympiapublishers.com
OLYMPIA PAPERBACK EDITION

A CIP catalogue record for this title is
available from the British Library.

ISBN: 978-1-80439-243-0

This is a work of fiction.
Names, characters, places and incidents originate from the writer's
imagination. Any resemblance to actual persons, living or dead, is
purely coincidental.

First Published in 2023

Olympia Publishers
Tallis House
2 Tallis Street
London
EC4Y 0AB

Printed in Great Britain

Acknowledgements

Thank you to my mum and dad for the never-ending support they have given me.

Part One

Introductions

Hello there, you do not know me yet, but you will in time my name is Zari Kingston. I am eighteen years old about five-foot-seven, I have a slim figure with brunette hair with natural highlight that make my emerald eyes stand out. My life hasn't been the easiest but I've lived through it the pain, loss and tragedy are all a large part but they shaped my life.

There is just one minor detail we are missing about me; when I was sixteen there was an accident which gave me and my twin special abilities. I got the ability to shapeshift into anyone, resurrect the dead, control a mass amount of power, and see the future. My brother got the ability to control fire, earth, weather and was able to read people's minds.

You will soon know more about me so shall we find out more about my life journey.

School

School was not the easiest thing for me as I got bullied and picked on for being different before the accident that happened to me. Not many people at school knew about what I was so I was considered as a freak like in P.T. Barnum's circus. When I told my brothers about the bullying, they did not believe me, but I did have a few people who stood by me.

There was big boy Cody, he was nice but could get annoying from time to time; his hair was the colour of light-yellow paper; it was the same as Cat's and Charlie's. Cat/Cody was skinnier than big boy and would always brighten your day, his laugh always brought a smile on my face. There was also Lennon, he had a crush on me since year two and still does; he has grey hair, he got picked on the same as me, but I always had his back and helped him stand up to the bullies. The reason he got picked on was because people couldn't understand what he was saying so I helped him out. Then finally, there was Charlie; he always had a grin on his face his laugh was just like a monkey he was always there for me when I was down.

However, this year was just about to get harder as we had our final exams preparing us for our GSCE'S in year eleven so we had a year to prepare ourselves (we were in year ten). On September the 16th, it was a cold autumn day, I was sitting with the guys for break when the 'cool kids' came over.

"Hey Zari, why are you so weird and why do your eyes change, why do you have no parents?" one of them called out.

Why can't these airheads leave me alone? I thought to myself.

"Why does your family have mutt smell?" another retorted.

That's it! No one throws insults towards my family! I screamed in my head, causing me to stand face to face with the group of boys with my fists clenched my nails piercing into my skin. On many occasions I stood up to the boys, but this time it was different; I could sense that the wolf side was wanting to attack for insulting my family. I began to growl; my emerald eyes turned into dust gold. The fear of the boys radiating was clearly visible.

With all the strength Charlie had, he tried to pull me back into my chair as he could see the fear growing in their eyes.

They soon made a runner and said, "We will never mess with you again," and ran off to safety.

As I sat down in my chair Charlie gave me a tight hug to try and calm me down, I was reluctant, but I hugged him back and my once gold eyes turned back to their emerald colour.

After a second, we pulled back from the hug.

Charlie enquired, "Why don't we have some hot chocolate?"

In unison we all said, "Sure," we laughed for a minute while Charlie was asking me if I want hot chocolate, he shook his head.

"I was only asking Z but we all might as well have some," he responded with a large grin on his face and walked off to the drinks stand.

We laughed again; the guys knew about me being a shifter they did not think I was weird but special and unique. They were the best people I knew.

After a few moments of waiting, Charlie came back with five cups of hot chocolate with whipped cream and marshmallows, I was surprised he got the full hot chocolate not just the drink.

"You are a legend, Charlie! Thanks," I exclaimed with a grin on my face I leaned over and kissed him on the cheek as another thank you, he chuckled awkwardly and blushed as red as a tomato which made the guys and I laugh. As we drank our hot chocolate, I couldn't help but notice the large grin on his face, I just shrugged it off and thought nothing of it.

Once we finished our cup of hot chocolate, we heard the bell signalling us to go to third lesson.

"What have you guys got again?" I asked

"You and Charles have science. Me, Lennon and Thompson have maths with Ms Weberfeild," Cody replied in a deep voice and rolling his eyes when he said, 'Ms Weberfeild'.

Everyone hated Ms Weberfeild because she couldn't actually teach us. How she got the job of a math teacher I don't know but luckily, I had Mr Perry, he was a really good teacher, but he always let us out late to our next class.

As me and Charlie were walking towards science class, we came across a strange looking person who we had never seen before. Who was he?

Bretherstone

We saw a boy who looked like a transfer student but where was he from? Who was he? Me and Charlie walked into class where we met Theo or Astro boy; he was into astrophysics so much it got on your nerves. He had a slightly pale face with brown eyes and brown hair, and he was shorter than me.

"Aww aren't you two the cutest couple," Theo said with a chuckle and a devilish grin plastered in his face.

"I told you, Theo, we are not a couple, and you know I don't do relationships or any lovey-dovey stuff that's just disgusting," I replied in a husky voice and pretending to fake gag.

"Theo, who's the new kid?" Charlie asked in a curious voice.

"Oh, that boy the mysterious one," Theo said pointing at the new boy who had light brown hair with silver eyes that shone in the sun like polished iron.

I gave Theo a death glare, "Theo don't make accusations and no finger pointing."

Theo just a had a little laugh; he always knew how to annoy me.

"His name is Ollie Bretherstone, he came from America. Apparently, his parents got put in prison for mad science experiments, kind of creepy don't you think?" Theo said finally answering the question.

"I'm going to go and talk to him and if you try to stop me Theo, I will tell Thea Nightheart that you like her." The boys sighed knowing that they wouldn't be able to stop me from telling

Theo's crush that he likes her. I knew how to threaten people and apparently, I was scary.

I picked up my bag and book and went over to the transfer student. I tried to greet him kindly by offering my hand to shake and introduce myself.

"Hi, I'm Zari do you mind if I join you?" I asked politely.

"No, not at all. I'm Ollie you have a beautiful name, Zari."

"Thanks," I replied with a little blush, he noticed and laughed a little. He didn't seem anything like his parent from what I read about them in the news.

We were doing chemistry in class combining elements to create compounds. Ollie was exceptional at it, well he would be, his parents probably taught him how to make dangerous substances. I glanced over to see how Theo and Charlie were doing. Charlie had soot all over his face while Theo had slime over his face, I giggled, Ollie saw what I was looking at and let out a small chuckle.

"Those your friends?" he asked

"Unfortunately, they are. They are so annoying at times but can be funny," I replied. "Why?"

"You seem too cute and beautiful for guys like that are you like one of the popular girls?" he said whilst tucking a piece of hair behind my ear.

"No," I replied in a sad tone. "I get bullied every day because I'm not really normal."

"Do you know what my cousin would say? She would say that if you were normal, you would be boring but if you were unique and special like yourself you are extraordinary."

"Your cousin seems very wise and kind," I replied with a faint smile on my face.

Just as he was about to say something, the bell rang

signalling us to go to next lesson, he had the same lesson as me and the guys so went down to history.

During the lessons me and Ollie got closer and became friends. He was very nice and after our class had finished, we headed to lunch. Ollie said he would head to the library to do a bit of studying while I went to go and talk to the other boys, they had two spare seats anticipating that Ollie was going to join us, but I had told them everything that me and Ollie had talked about.

"Shall we go to dodgeball practice guys?" Cat/Cody asked, we all nodded our heads in agreement.

When we were heading down, we passed Ollie and asked if he wanted to come and join us at dodgeball and he agreed he was quite a good player. When practice had finished, we all had a free lesson but when I had a free lesson at the end of the day, I would leave so that I could get away from everyone and be by myself, let out all of my frustration, most of all, be free. Today it was only me and Behrad who had a free lesson, so we left school and went to the forest of Sawadro.

Family

In my life I knew there was my family who I could count on to help me with everything; help me suppress the side of me I tried to hide, be there at the lowest point of my life. My family may be broken but we would count on each other.

I have two brothers, my twin brother Behrad and my older brother Jake. Behrad has ear-length black hair with deep-sea-blue eyes, he is the same height as me but has a slightly broader figure, but he does have a funny side which makes him do stupid things for no reason. There was this one time in primary where he put toothpaste over nearly everything the teacher owned which landed him a detention for three months. My brother Jake is quite different from my twin, Behrad; he doesn't fool around as much as him, but he does from time to time. He has a strong, broad figure with jet-black hair which make his ocean-blue eyes stand out, he is about five-foot-eleven. Jake can get quite overprotective over me and Behrad in any situation. My parents were not always the best, when I was five my mom was killed and after her death my father turned to drinking to drown his sorrows and wasn't able to help me and my brothers, so Jake became a father figure for me and Behrad.

If you think that it is about my life, well, you're wrong, my family are what you call half-wolf or shifters. A half-wolf is a person who is born with wolf DNA whereas a werewolf is bitten and given wolf DNA. Any family that are half-wolf derive from wolf tribes dating back to the 11th century. We can turn into our wolf forms at will, not when there is a full moon like a werewolf, so we can change when we are angry, sad or anything. Everyone has unique colouring except people who have a twin, but you have some differences between the two. Jake's is dark brown, father's is black, my mother's was pure white, mine and Behrad's is light brown, but I have white ears whereas Behrad has brown ears. People ask do you change people into werewolves, the answer is no; we change people if they are close to death, but we give them the choice to live or die. There are many half-wolves who change people for no reason, and they are considered as the rouge wolves. My family are not put into any category as we don't follow many of the rules of the wolf community except the most major rules:

-    Keep the shifter existence from humans.
-    Only change people in life-or-death situations.

We abide by our own rules, so we are considered as an alone pack.

The Accident

It was two days before my sweet sixteenth birthday. It was December the 1st (mine and Behrad's birthday was on the 3rd of December), I had spent the day before with Charlie and the other guys while I was going to spend today with Ollie. Up to this point I had only known him for a few weeks. We became closer friends, but he did want to date me, so I rejected him and said that I am not one for relationships. He didn't seem to heartbroken about it, but we were still friends. He invited me over his house to do a study party and he was doing something special for my birthday which I kept questioning about whether something bad was going to happen.

I took in a deep breath before entering the house, he said I could walk straight in without knocking, I thought it was a bit weird, but somethings are strange even when we figure them out. As I walk in it felt strange the air felt thick as if something weren't right. There was a funny smell like chemicals shivers ran down my spine.

"Hello, Ollie, you there?" I call out as my breathing becomes heavy.

I sense someone creep up on me they grab me and place a cloth with a funny smell over my mouth and nose, muffling my screams, my breath soon becomes shallow, my eyes become tired, and everything goes black as I pass out.

As I regain consciousness my vision is still blurred but I can make out a figure. Who is he? I look over and see that I am strapped to a draft table and see another person attached to one. Who is he?

Soon my vision completely comes back to me, and I see that the other person that is strapped down to the table is Behrad. He is still unconscious; they must have got him when he was on his way to the cemetery. I hear an evil masculine laugh.

"Who are you? What do you want with me and my brother? Let my brother go!" I call out to the figure hiding in the shadows.

"Oh, do you not recognize me Zari, or should say Z, you were wrong that I am nothing like my parents but I don't make mistakes like them I need test subjects to try out my new serum and as you said you were bullied and that no one would care if you and your brother disappeared," he said while stepping out of the shadows revealing himself and letting out an evil chuckle at the end of his speech.

"Ollie what are you doing to us?" I ask him in a stern voice.

"Oh, I am going to make more than an ordinary person by adding something into your bloodstream and you're going to get to witness it, but your brother will be knocked out until you leave here."

He walks back over to the lab table with bubbling chemicals and matter of things that only a mad science person would know about. But just as he was about to get everything prepared someone comes in.

"Oliver, there are people here what do you want us to do?"

"Give me a minute, Roy, let me get everything ready for this to go off then we will send the people off and leave as the chemicals will not be stable, these two will likely be killed in the process, so get everybody rounded up. I'll deal with the people out front."

"Okay Ollie where do you want us to meet you? At the

well?"

He nodded, I began to get worried as Jake doesn't know where we are and what will happen to us; when those chemicals go off my breathing increases as I start to pace in my head.

All the chemicals begin going critical as Ollie has everything prepared for the experiment to go off, I notice a clock that say two minutes, I guessed that it was the time left before I meet my death. Ollie walks over to me and grabs my face in his hand with a tight grip.

"I wish things could be different between us, but this has to happen, it's destiny. He said it would happen, that we would be battling for years but if this didn't happen, time would collapse, and we would not have life and everything would be broken," he says as if this was my fate for me to die or for this to happen.

He lets go of my face and walks away to the door and disappears, I keep my eyes on the device as it counts down, I glance at my brother I wish we had more time. What were father and Jake going to be like if me and Behrad had died? Just as I take a deep breath, I become unconscious.

The next thing I know I am on the floor, pain rushes through my body, headaches overwhelm my head as I start to see things that might happen in the future. All I think about is getting my brother home, I use all the strength I had left to get up and make my way over to my brother and take him home.

I take the route through the cemetery as it is the quickest route, I stare at the grave my eyes widen as dead bodies come out of the ground, I take my eyes off of them and look back; the ground has risen a little but there was no one there. I turn my focus back to Behrad, I drag him home when I find Jake and Father running over to me and my twin; my father takes Behrad. Once he takes Behrad everything becomes black, but I feel a pair

23

of strong arms lift me up and bring me towards the house.

As I begin to wake up my head still feels fuzzy, I slowly get up with pain everywhere but use my strength to get up. I find that I am in the sitting room with a note beside me, it was from Ollie.

Zari,

I see that you made it out alive you must be in pain now; I will tell you what abilities you and your brother have think of this as a gift.

Your abilities are shapeshifting, seeing the future, resurrecting the dead, and controlling a mass amount of power. A likely killer.

Behrad's abilities are to control fire, earth, weather and read people's mind. A saviour.

Are you going to tell them that you and Behrad are dangerous? If your brother doesn't know he won't be dangerous as his powers won't kick in until he knows. You however, you won't have a choice what are going to do with your life?

I will hunt you down because you are dangerous, you can kill someone with a snap of your fingers, and I will be a hero. Run Zari, Run.

Bye, bye.

Ollie.

I have no choice, but I must go on the run, make myself disappear so that I can protect my family. They shouldn't be harmed for my mistakes, where will I go; I'll have to travel the world, stay low, stay close to the shadows.

Slowly I crept towards my room, left a note saying 'you will never see me again'. Pack a load of clothes into a small backpack and left all my precious items I dressed in a black leather jacket and a pair of black skinny fit leggings to match my black top. I climbed out the window and ran towards the woods I ran as fast as I could and jumped across the cliff and transformed into my wolf while in the air. I looked back at the house. I let out a howl with a tear in my eye and ran off into the forest never to be seen again.

Running

From the ages of sixteen and eighteen I was on the run from Bretherstone. He has tried to hunt me down because after what he said in the lab that we would be fighting for years I knew that there would be battle waiting to happen. I have always been able to stay one step ahead from them with my ability to see the future. I did end with many battle scars, with broken bones but learnt new ways to fight. Whilst I was on the run I was known as Iona Sclater or Brodie Morgan.

I have been using my shapeshifting ability to blend in with the crowd. I made many new acquaintances along the way, I helped them in many ways that they all say that the owe me something, but I said I'll see you again one day.

I have travelled every corner of the globe running, I have been to some horrific places and some magnificent places.

I stayed in Britain till the end of December so that I get an idea of what it would be like on the run. I learnt not to keep contact with anyone. Change your identity every so often. Trust no one.

January 1997—Moscow was the first place I visited, the snow falls never ended, it was beautiful. I met Benjamin there, he was brilliant with sword fighting. He taught me how to fight with swords. But during my training we got ambushed there and I saved his life and helped his family escape.

He says that he will repay the favour one day I said, "You don't need to."

February 1997—After Moscow I went to the North China sea where I met Ping. He was an exceptional cook; the food was amazing and in return I helped him start his cooking career. I left making sure that his family was safe so that Ollie's band of merry men would never come after them. Ping says that we will meet again sometime in the future.

March 1997—Next, I travelled to the island which holds a place where people learn how to become assassins, they welcomed me, but I said that it was only a temporary arrangement that they agreed on. Training with people, that was difficult as you always have to watch your back. When we were attacked from Ollie, I was just able to save everyone, but I walked away with some new scars.

April 1997—New Zealand was my next destination; I was able to stay there longer than a month as I had the New Zealand government behind me. They said I was able to stay there for the rest of my life, but I didn't want to put a whole country at risk, I didn't want anybody at risk for what I have done.

June 1997—I travelled to South Africa where I met some local villagers where I helped them gather many resources, they were incredibly grateful. I was glad nothing bad happened to them I stayed with the peaceful villagers; they were not warriors but simple people.

July 1997—Over the summer I travelled across Africa in July. I came across a village in Zambia, they were poor and did not own very much, like in South Africa. I helped them get many resources to help them in daily life. I taught the children a bit and they were very grateful for my gifts for their hospitality.

August 1997—I came across a village in Zambezi with people who were fighters, but they had pure hearts they were incredible people. My friend, Amaya, she was amazing, she taught me many ways to fight. When it came to the end of the second month of staying in the village, Ollie found me, I was able to protect the village, but I was injured badly. My wounds would heal in time. I left the village with them saying that they were in my debt, I smiled and walked away from the village.

October 1997—Sudan was in war, but I was able to help the people find peace by making their rivalling countries equals so that the war was over and that many lives were not lost.

November 1997—Egypt was beautiful, all the mummies and tombs and the great pyramids were a beautiful sight I was in awe at everything I saw. I passed the river Nile many days whilst in Egypt. Learning hieroglyphics was not easy but now I know more than when I was in school.

December 1997—Syria was ravished by war; everywhere I looked there was pain and suffering, this had been going on for years, but I could not help as it would attract too much attention. Or Ollie would find me. It was a hard year being away from my family, they probably thought I was dead. Behrad was probably a ghost as he was always glum when I wasn't around, like the time I was attacked and in a coma for two months.

January 1998—Iraq wasn't that much different from Syria. The two countries were at war, I tried my hardest to stay in the shadows. I was able to give people food and other resources. I helped many people, but I could not cease the war. Many times, in Syria and Iraq, I was found in the middle of an attack I was able to save the injured and children. I only walked away with a few flesh wounds but nothing too severe that would need much attention. The last time I saw Ollie was in Zambezi.

February 1998—Austria was cold but beautiful, the mountains were an amazing sight and at night the northern lights were just incredible. However, the beautiful sight was ruined when Ollie showed up, we fought old school; I gave him a few cuts and bruises.

March 1998—Italy was stunning! The canals were always running, the food was divine. While on my travels through Italy I came across a man named Joey. He taught me how to make traditional Italian dishes while I helped him to collect a mass number of clams. He also wanted to learn how to fight so I taught some simple moves, nothing like on the island in the North China sea.

April 1998—Spain was lovely and warm I received a dark suntan the food there was astonishing. The paella was to die for. While I was in Spain, I met this man named Paulo, he taught me how to speak many languages. When I was in other countries I rarely spoke and only spoke to people who could speak English. I was taught Spanish, French, Italian, Russian, Polish, Chinese and many other languages.

June 1998—Cuba was not what I expected. I thought there would be simple people like in Africa, but they were artists. Their parades were magnificent, the dancing was so fast and majestic. I was like how can they move their feet that fast it was like tango mixed with tap dancing. Although while at one of the festivals, Ollie absolutely trashed the decorations, I made sure that everyone was at safety but before I could start a fight with Ollie he was gone.

July 1998—Mexico. I tried my hardest to lay low and stay away from everyone every night after the Cuba incident. I read the letter that Ollie sent me again, 'I will hunt you down' always ran through my mind. Maybe he was right, maybe I am a killer I could have caused hundreds of people to die that day at the festival if I fought Ollie. But instead, I chose to save their lives so maybe I am not a killer but a saviour a protector.

August 1998—Bermuda was a small island, so while I was there, I quite often climbed the hillside and practised the fighting techniques I have been taught over the past months. I thought that maybe I could stay there forever, but living in this beautiful place, it would be like purgatory without my family.

September 1998—Canada was cold and had blustering winds. Temperatures would drop from cold to freezing. Most countries I have been to it has been cold, but nothing like Canada. I still stayed close to the shadows, no one was ever going to get hurt because of me. I trusted Ollie when I had a gut feeling that something was going to go wrong. Luckily, I was safe in North America as Ollie and his 'minions' were permanently banned from the continent, I had one thing that was dawning on me about the United States, but what?

USA

From October, I was in America I was being drawn to New York City, but I didn't know what it was.

In around early November I travelled towards New York City where I came across a person who was about nineteen years old who looked exactly the same as Jake, but he was taller I couldn't help myself but think it was Jake, so I walked up the young stranger.

"Hello, sorry, but do I know you Sir?" I asked as politely as I could.

"I'm not sure but you look familiar to me do you know a lady called Sara Kingston?"

How does he know my mum maybe his parents were related to mum? "Yeah, I do she is my mum, why do you ask?" I replied in a questioning look, he looked at me with his jaw dropped and eyes wide.

"It's just um—well—a few days ago I was curious about my family as I was adopted fourteen years ago and um—I took a test, and it came back with my real parents Sara and Jimmy Kingston and apparently, I have a twin brother named Jake. Oh, why am I so stupid, I haven't even introduced myself, my name is Jax."

I look at him in awe I knew my father had secrets but nothing like this, an older brother and the twin to Jake. Millions of questions ran through my mind like why he was given away. Why was I never told about Jax?

"Sorry, my name is Zari, do you know anywhere not out in

31

the open, like somewhere private?" I asked, looking around.

"Of course, follow me," he said with a smile just like Jake's; it broke my heart into a million pieces. He gave me his hand and he led the way.

As he showed me the way he led me towards a night club I thought *why were we going to a night club in the middle of the day?* We entered the building where I saw three other boys, they all seemed to be related. Two of them were identical but one a little shorter than the other they both had brown hair with light brown eyes that were like milk chocolate, they both had small, broad figures, nothing like my brothers'. The other boy was a lot shorter than the other two with a bowl cut brown hairstyle. I giggle at little at the hair; he seemed quite skinny. When Jax saw me giggle he let out a small smirk

The twins seemed to be staring at me as if I were a god, who I found highly amusing and confusing at the same time. I haven't been like this in two years, it felt different and good in a way.

"Hey, Jax who's the hot chick?" called out one of the twins.

"Hey Frankie, keep your hands off my little sister. Mickie stop drooling over her," Jax replied backing them of away from me when he said I was his sister they had their eyes wide as if they were going to pop out. I laughed at their facial expressions of confusion and amazement.

"I didn't know you have a sister and when were you going to tells us?" the other twin said.

"I only found out today, but I think my sister needs to know who you are before she gives you embarrassing nicknames. The one on the right is Frankie. The one in the middle is Mickie—"

"Bowl cut over here is Tommy or shorty. Call him whatever you want," Mickie called out as he interrupted Jax. I let out a quiet giggle as Mickie shouted out the names. The boys smirked at me as I covered my face with hands and I was blushing extremely hard.

"Hey!" I heard tommy call out halfway through my embarrassing moment.

After a few moments I calmed down and I introduce myself to the boys.

"Hi, I'm Zari, do you mind if I catch up with my brother a bit as I haven't seen him for fourteen years. Also, do you mind if I stay here?"

"You can stay here as long as you like little sis, there's a spare room you can use and I'm just saying that on a Tuesday and a Thursday, we run a night club."

I nod my head in understanding that things could get a bit loud on those days. After I nod my head, Jax extends his arm directing towards the staircase. I follow him up the staircase to a private room where me and Jax catch up on the fourteen years we have lost. When I told him about mum's death, he seemed quite disheartened. We talked for hours until Tommy came in saying that the alcohol delivery had come in. Jax said he would be back in a minute.

After he went to collect the liquor, I decided I would have an exploration of the place where I found four bedrooms, a spare room and a liquor room. I saw the boys carrying boxes towards the storage room. I climbed down the stairs as they were waving off to the truck driver. They turned around to look at me; Frankie and Mickie still had their jaws dropped at me.

"Hey twin boys stop jaw dropping at me or I'll punch you," I told the two boys in a stern voice, I looked around and I couldn't see Tommy. "Where's Tommy?" I asked.

"He said he was going to look through newspaper articles because he thought he had seen you before from somewhere."

33

Mickie replied.

Just as Mickie had finished his answer Tommy came barging through with a newspaper from December the 3rd 1996, my heart begins to race.

"You remember that girl from Britain who disappeared who was involved in accident a day before she disappeared and who is the daughter of your father who has been presumed dead for the past two years! It is your sister Jax, her," Tommy blurted out whilst panting from running quickly.

"You're right Tommy." The boys shot shocked expressions, "Two years ago, I was involved in an accident which gave me some abilities and I am also a half-wolf like you are Jax I ran away because the person who caused the accident is hunting me. You know when Cuba was attacked in June? That was his doing," I said telling them the full truth.

"So Behrad my little brother also has abilities like you?"

I nodded.

"Why didn't you stay with them?"

"I had to make sure they were protected and not in danger for my mistakes. The man who is hunting me has caused this, his parents are the scientists Mr and Mrs Bretherstone." They looked at me in shock, they could see and hear that I was tearing up Jax came straight over to me and engulfed me in a hug. He held me in the hug while I cried into his shoulder, he stroked my hair trying to calm me down.

After a few moments I calmed down, they asked if I wanted anything, but I shook my head and said that I was going to go up and have a lie down. A few hours later I woke up to find Jax sitting on the bed and he smiled at me. I lazily got out of the bed changed my clothes, I followed Jax downstairs to find that it was night and I saw the boys had a dinner all set up and tried to make me laugh I just smirked at them.

Between November and December, I taught the boys how defend themselves like a person from the place where I was trained, they got quite a few bruises and cuts and they couldn't believe that I was a better fighter than them. They could just fight back and defend themselves but the thought that I had abandoned my family made my heart ache.

On December the 13th the boys and me decided that we would go to Britain and see my family to give them the truth to what actually happened to me. I was scared about what their reaction would be, but Jax gave me hope and I wondered what Father would be like when he saw Jax.

Millions of things ran through my head before I knew my breathing had become shallow, the last thing I saw was Tommy and Jax rushing towards me before everything went black.

Later I woke up in the room I was using and found all the boys crowded around me they we all asked me if I was all right, I just nodded and said that we'd better get going to England.

Home

On December the 15th we arrived at my old home. Ever since I have been on the run, I have had nowhere to call home and where I used to live, I called my old home. The brothers went to a hotel area where they were going to be staying while me and Jax walked up to the home that Jax was going to go to first. We stopped a few metres away from the house Jax nodded at me and walked to the front door; I couldn't hear what they were saying but father seemed so happy to have his son back my brothers and their goofy faces looked so confused.

After a few moments, Jax turned around and gave me the signal to come. I took in a deep breath to calm my nerves; nervous I walked towards the house and I came out of the shadows. All of them except Jax had shocked expressions on their faces. Father rushed over to me and asked if it really was me, he had tears in his eyes I guess he probably would be after getting two of his children back after thinking they were both dead.

We all got together to have a family moment. The last time since we had a family moment like this was on my fourth birthday fourteen years ago. After the touching moment we walked inside the house. I don't know why but I hesitated I think it was because I abandoned my home to protect them; just as I was having second thoughts about coming home to my family, I turned to see Behrad who had a reassuring hand on my shoulder; I smiled at him having a tear in my eye he brought up his free hand to my face and used his thumb to wipe away the tear.

We laughed when we heard father shouting at us to hurry up looking at each other we smiled and walked into the spare room and caught up on everything that happened over the last few years.

After about an hour of talking I had a vision, it was flashing through mind; I could just about grasp that there were people here and a bomb.

As loud as I could at the top of my lungs I shouted, "Get down!" In that split second before the actual bomb went off everyone was able to get down with just a few scratches. I quickly jumped back onto my feet and made sure that they were all okay, there was a small sigh of relief.

"Get out of here! I'll handle them while you lot get safety don't argue with me, now. Now, go!" I told them.

They nodded and left the house and headed towards a safe place I looked and then turned back round with determination to get these people who tried to attack my family. I blocked off the exit with heavy objects using my power to control a mass amount of something making sure no one could escape the direction that my family did.

Rage was coursing through my veins, people having targeted my family waiting for me to come home; I sensed other wolves around I shift into my form, and I find six other wolves. They all growl in my direction, one at a time they tried to attack me eventually I am fighting them all at once. I am just able to attack them and knock them out; a small wave of relief comes over me, but I know it's not the end.

When I walk out to the front garden area, I find that I am up against thirty-two people. I find two knifes, I pick up the knifes and use the techniques that Benjamin taught me.

"Let's say you take it easy on me boys, make it fair." I give them a small smirk after a moment or two they come straight at me one against thirty-two, I didn't like those odds.

Fighting that many guys at once was not easy but I was able to fend them off for long enough. I got hit quite a few times but in the bushes, I noticed a bow and arrows. I thought of Jax he said he quite often took archery lessons. I used my ability to control things to make the bow come to me. I shot about twelve of them with arrows; ten I was able to get with the knifes, ten left to go. I ditched the weapons but the bow and used that to hit them with; five were left. I had been lucky with the other twenty-seven guys but these five were truly skilled I was getting hit at more often, it wasn't until someone started shooting bullets at three of the men then it started getting easier. Up against the last two who were killing me; with every punch I was getting weaker. It wasn't until the guy on the left stabbed my right side, did I finally give up. The two guys got shot except for the person who shot the other three. I crashed to the floor gasping for air.

I had lost hope and thought that the guy with the gun was going to kill me, but he wasn't, it was Jax.

"Stay with me Zari, stay with me. We need to get you out of here. Keep your eyes open don't close them on me, okay."

I nod my head in understanding, "I thought Ollie would be the one to kill me but at least I might be able to spend my last moments with my brother," I was saying through gasps of air as I could feel my lungs having trouble collecting oxygen.

"Don't say that we have just got you back now if you have any pain just try to relax all right."

I nod my head, not knowing what he was trying to do.

"Ready, one—two—three—" he lifted me into his arms and carried me towards the hospital or somewhere; every so often I could feel my eyes getting heavy and wanting to close, but Jax told me to stay awake.

Once we arrived, I was taken to an operating room. I could see father, Jake and Behrad looking at me in worry and many other emotions. I woke up a couple of hours later in a hospital with my family looking at the floor anxiously. I was just able to get the strength to speak a little, but I had pain coursing through my body like a drug.

"Hey," I was able to say in a low quiet voice.

They all looked at me as if I were aghast.

"Thank God you're awake," Jake said in a relieved tone and came over to hug me, but I let out a groan in pain.

"You have twelve bruised ribs, two broken ribs, a punctured lung, a stab in your right side and a mild concussion. Why the hell did you try to take them on all on your own?" Father said in a serious tone.

"I was trying to protect you, I know I have a lot of secrets, and some are way too dangerous for you to know, all my life you have looked after me so now let me protect you from the danger that I have locked myself in," I replied in an annoyed tone.

"Oh, so you say, leaving us for two years without even saying goodbye or even a scrap of something to say where you were for two years, we thought you were dead and now you are close to death and you're not even telling us the reason behind all of this," he retaliated back with a strong frown on his face.

"Dad, stop!" Behrad said in a calm voice trying to calm Father down.

"No Behrad when you two came back from something, your sister was the only one who knew what happened; you only remember getting attacked and then waking up in the house whereas your sister was awake and was carrying you back to the house then goes missing for two years and then the minute she gets back to the house an explosion goes off and then thirty-eight men turn up and your sister fights them off and almost gets herself killed in the process, so I want you to tell us the full truth, not the lies that have you been telling us!" he bellowed back showing his full anger.

"You want the full truth Dad. Fine. Well, you're not going to like it, okay. You remember that boy Ollie? Well he created something, and he kidnapped me and Behrad to test it on and there was an explosion which gave me and Behrad abilities. I didn't tell Behrad because I didn't want him to think that he was dangerous, but he was given a choice to know about them, but I wasn't. Over the last two years I have been on the run from Ollie as he has been hunting me down! Do you know the attack in Cuba? That was caused by him, and I didn't want to put you lot in danger, so I have been trying to protect you from my mistakes. There you go, there's the full story," I replied answering my father, they all looked astonished at what I had just told them.

I have been trying to keep them safe, but they won't see that it's for their own good they all took in the information; my father had to sit back down in the chair trying to process everything I had said, he seemed quite taken back on the information.

"Why didn't you tell me?" Behrad said, breaking the silence.

"I didn't tell you because I didn't want you to fear yourself your entire life you had a choice, I didn't. Only once you know fully about your abilities will you be able to access them, I couldn't let my brother be afraid all his life," I replied back to him with a tear in my eye.

"We are the ones who are supposed to protect you you're not supposed to protect us you're the youngest of us we already lost mom we don't need to lose you too," Jake called out in a saddened voice.

"You lot should go somewhere safe. Jax, in my bag there should be a set of house keys," I said breaking the silence. Jax nodded and walked over to my bag to rummage through and found a set of keys.

"What do we need these for?" Jake asked in a questionable tone.

"You are going to go to a house which I have, and you are going to stay there until I come and tell you it's safe, don't argue with me, this is for your own good," As I was saying my sentence, I started to think about mum and just a few seconds after I had finished ordering my brothers around a white figure appeared.

All of them looked spellbound; it was Mum, Father just kept stuttering.

"Believe in our daughter, Jimmy she is trying to keep you safe and let her keep you safe," my mother said in a quiet but wise voice.

My father had a tear in his eye, we had never seen our father cry before, but he nodded at what the ghost said she gave a smile towards all of us she disappeared like smoke blowing away.

"All right Zari, we'll go to the house just promise me you won't get yourself killed," Father spoke up in a sincere voice.

I nodded, he kissed my forehead and told the boys that they would see me later and I promised them that I would make it home alive. They walked out towards the door and gave me a smile, they all had tears in their eyes, but they left. After they left, I had a sigh of relief that they were going to be safe.

Preparation

After three weeks of being in a hospital bed, recovering, I was ready for what fate had in store for me. I grabbed out my new gear which Theo had made for me, I told him that the reason I had left for two years was that I got a job opportunity, and they believed it. They came to visit me nearly all the time, which I appreciated after missing them so much.

One day while I was recovering Jake came to me and told me that I was like *Batman,* apparently it was going round like viral, and he said, "Zari you have inspired me to become a better person and you're my hero. I made this for you, I think you should be a hero and inspire people and make a change to the world."

He handed me a black mask, I looked at him and I knew he wanted me to become more than just who I am.

The day I was leaving hospital I decided that I would visit a rundown place I used to go to as a kid. It was a six-mile walk from the hospital, the place was an industrial factory, but it went bust in 1989 so we went there to play around; Dad would get so scared where we were.

"Figured you'd come here." I turned around and saw Jake standing there with a smug look on his face.

"Why are you here I told you to stay at the bunker until I came," I retaliated at him in a stern voice.

His once joyous face turned into a frown, he looked like I had done something wrong, but I was only trying to protect him and keep him safe.

"You need to leave before I kick you out and send you in a parcel back to Dad saying to restrain all of you for coming after me so make your decision Jake or I will," I shout at him for not answering me.

"I am not leaving my little sister throwing herself into a death trap then leaving to disappear again. I lost Mom I am not losing my only sister, so I am going to stay here and fight with you even if it kills me, I will fight till my last breath."

I take all of his words processing them thinking about what he said.

"If you are going to stay here then stay with me you need to learn a few things and here is my other condition. You will learn a few things and do as I say and learn a few fighting techniques and become a side man like the getaway driver, and you will only take down a few people and if anything gets too heated you will leave, is that understood?" I said with a strong tone to show that I will not adjust.

"Deal, you have my word but promise me one thing, don't get yourself killed."

I nod my head, but I know that, that promise I won't be able to keep.

Over the next twenty days I taught my brother what he needed to know about my techniques I showed him no mercy not even the slightest, during the sessions he kept begging for a break, but I told him that when you face your enemies, they give no mercy or breaks. He soon learned. He wanted a code name so I gave him the black cub similar to his wolf one of the advantages of being part wolf you can run fast and attack with a lot more force.

"Sis when are we going to face Bretherstone and actually

defeat the guy who caused my sister pain?" he asked with anger and impatience in his voice.

I wasn't facing him as I was sharpening a couple of weapons, I could tell he wanted to get justice for the last two years of pain.

"Why do you want to get him so bad? Is it because you want to get justice for what happened to me but if you want to get him so badly then you are going to have to leave, I didn't ask for your help, you wanted to help I didn't want you here this is my fight so you might as well leave if you want to kill Bretherstone yourself," I retaliated at him.

He could see that I was mad at him, and I could see the regret in his eyes for what he had said to me, and I didn't want him there if he was going to be selfish like that. To get Bretherstone wasn't his fight, it was mine and was always going to be till the day I die.

"I know where you're coming from. But there is something you should know. When you left for two years Charlie the boy you were around with, he was torn to pieces he loved you and he still hasn't moved on, he still believes that you're dead he put his life on hold for you."

I could feel the tears in my eyes, I had abandoned loads of people that day I left I didn't want them to be in harm's way. I know that I should have said something, but I didn't I chose to pretend to be dead for two years I wanted them to forget about me and move on from me.

"I'm not leaving you, I have missed you for two years and it made me see all the regrets I made throughout my life you are not leaving the picture you are my hero, sis and I want to pay you back." As he said his little speech, he placed his large hands on my shoulders and pulled me into a hug while I just thought about what I had done wrong for leaving for two years.

44

The next ten days were spent with more training but on March the 13th he was finally ready for what our destiny had in store for us. He chose to go for the gun while I went with metal rods and knives but at least he wasn't fighting like I was, he was going to be a sniper. I was in black leather clothing while he was in marine clothing.

On March the 15th we were attacked by twelve guys and I thought this was a good experience for what was to come he had a good kick at it, he walked away with few stitches but he got about five while I got the rest.

"Not bad for a first try, Jake, come on, you did really well and to be honest with you I think you're ready for what the future holds," I told him while doing his stitches; he wouldn't stop making moaning sounds and grunting.

"Really? Only a few days ago you said you didn't want me here. Ow! When did you learn how to clean up wounds?" he replied, still in pain.

"Quit your moaning, I learnt how to while I was with the league, and I was wrong I do think that you can be a big help and you are my brother."

"Thanks, you'll always be my little sis even if you're a better fighter, a badass, a genius, a doctor, a person who can speak ten languages and many other things, you may be more powerful but you're my little sis and I'll always protect you."

I laughed at his little speech about what I was, better than him; with open arms he dragged me into a bone crushing hug. That was when I thought only a few more days of training and he'll be ready for what fate has in store for us.

Every day the question remained in the back of my mind, who was Ollie talking about, what did he mean by that this had to happen, who was trying to control our lives? Destiny is

45

supposed to be what we make, surely there it not a god controlling us all.

"What are you thinking about?" Jake said while he was standing behind me and causing me to jump up and put a knife to his throat. "Okay next time don't creep up on you if I don't want to risk getting my throat cut."

"Sorry league techniques. I was just thinking about what Ollie said the day I got my abilities he said, 'I wish things could be different between us but this has to happen, it's destiny he said it would happen, that we would be battling for years but if this didn't happen time would collapse and we would not have life and everything would be broken'. He said it as if this was my fate for me to die or for this to happen. I want to know who this godlike person is."

"Maybe he isn't anyone maybe Bretherstone was just trying to play with your mind, but I don't think we have much time left before we have to fight, have you seen the news?"

I agree with my brother then turn to the television.

"City crisis as son of the mad science people, Mr and Mrs Bretherstone, is demanding the woman in black that has been fighting his forces. City police cannot take down the young Bretherstone and his forces, I am pleading that if the woman in black is listening, please come and defeat this man who is trying to kill citizens, protect our city," The news reporters says to the public.

The words sink into my mind I thought that I needed to protect the people of this city maybe I am a hero and not a killer maybe this is my future to take him down and become something greater than just Zari Kingston.

"I think we should get ready for what lies ahead brother."

"Agreed, Black Angel."

"I like that Black Cub."

He smirked at the name, and I smirked back at him.

That was when we knew that we would not have much time. Just after our moment of discovering our new names I started to have a loud ringing noise in my ears as I started to see what was going to happen soon, I saw a dead corpse with blood all over his face and body. I couldn't see who it was but soon enough the image of the form in my mind was gone.

"Zari are you okay? What did you see?" Jake asked in a worried but calm voice.

"I saw someone dead, but I couldn't tell who it was, I-I-I recognize him, but I couldn't tell," I replied whilst trying to catch my breath.

"It's okay just breathe okay now go get some rest for once I'm bossing you around," he says trying to make me relax and laughs at the last part and I laugh back at him.

But I do as he says and head to the upstairs rooms with a sofa bed and try to rest before tomorrow, the day I would be fighting and have fate play out in my life.

I will defeat Ollie and make him pay for all the pain and suffering he has caused in my family, making me and Behrad an outsider and taking me away from my family, he will pay.

But now I am going to be known as someone else as the Black Angel and I will protect my home and this city. I am the Black Angel.

The Fight

March 17th was the day my life crashed.

It was morning we were prepping our weapons making sure we had enough ammo and anything else we needed but I couldn't shake off the vision I had the last two nights I had nightmares of the body every time I saw it the face was becoming clearer.

Just as I was starting to drown myself deeper into my thoughts almost irretrievable. "You almost ready Zari?" Jake said breaking my train of thought.

"Yeah, you?" I replied shaking all my worries away, trying to keep my focus.

"You seem like you have something troubling you, is it the vision?"

I nodded then sat down on the metal bench; we had kitted the hide out like a marine like base.

"I never did ask you how you channelled your powers?" he asked out of the blue. I looked at him with a questioning look.

"I met this person in the league his name was Ricardo, he taught me how to be one with my powers like when we have to be one with our wolf he died on that island, and it was my fault I shouldn't have stayed there," I told him wiping an unwanted tear from my eye using my thumb. "Anyways we better get going before Ollie terrorises the city."

He nodded at my last words.

With that we left the base and transformed into our wolf selves we travelled for miles and miles until we reached

Manchester, the journey was long, but we were able to keep a steady speed throughout the travel. When we arrived at the heart of the city we remained in our form for a while, we did it so that we could keep our identity from everyone until Bretherstone and his band of merry men arrived. Hundreds of people were running around us evacuating so that they weren't caught up in this mess.

Soon enough he arrived. "Oh, seems like we have the puppy dogs here; why don't you show yourself and fight me."

With the words said we looked at each other before shifting. "Don't remember this brother; new one or oh, this is Jake isn't it? Well let's see which one of us is stronger, but you should know that this will not be our last battle." After a moment of hard stare, he finally said, "Let's stop the chit chat."

Once those words were said all of the men started lunging at us, Jake started shooting bullets at the men who tried to attack him, and he was constantly having to reload he was doing so well, and he was battling like a true hero and a big brother. Like the person he is, I had hoped nothing bad would happen.

I, however, kept pulling punches everywhere and trying to make a pathway for me to get to Ollie. I was slowly able to. I was knocking them out I didn't want to kill them and become a killer but there was a couple of people I had to kill. Soon I had to make my way over to Jake as he was getting ambushed and surrounded.

"Jake! You okay?" I asked him after I had taken out most of the men.

"Yeah, I'm fine go get this man who has caused us pain," Jake said to me and nodded, I nodded back, using my powers to move people out of the way and made my way to Bretherstone.

"Well, if the beautiful Zari Kingston has finally met her fate," Ollie said to me as I reached him and what was left of his lieutenants.

I started to take on the two lieutenants, I recognize one of them, but I can't remember where from. Out the corner of my eye

I notice that Jake seems to be struggling with the men, but I can't lose Bretherstone, not when I am so close to defeating him.

Once I had taken down the two lieutenants, I face Bretherstone. "Looks like it's just you and me now," I say with a small smirk, and he smirks back at me. We start to fight but with the amount I had been fighting a could feel my muscles aching and needing to rest.

He hits me in the stomach and starts to hit me again and again and it's starting to take me down all of my energy is gone. "Seems like you're not as strong as you thought. But I will leave you to your pitiful suffering," he said and laughed. He grabs me by my throat, starting to choke me I can feel my airways seizing. "Maybe I should have stayed in that lab with you then maybe I could have gotten some abilities then it would have been ten times as easier to get you but that would be too easy," he laughs maliciously as he throws me towards a wall. I see him walk over to Jake his men start to leave.

"No!" I scream as I see Bretherstone a knife in hand and starts to fight my brother.

"Jake, get out of here, run!"

They continue fighting until Ollie is able to hit Jake, he is about to stab him his eyes widen as he runs the knife right through Jake's heart and I scream out in pain.

Jake drops to the floor choking. Ollie cleans his knife on the grass, places it back into its case and walks away.

"No! Jake!" I say in a sadden tone as I watched the man I had once trusted kill my brother right before my eyes and act like nothing and that Jake was just a nobody.

I felt my heart shatter to a million pieces it was like a part of my soul was attached to him and that I was losing a part of myself when he was choking, his death coming near. Time just stopped in that moment of his death; my heart ached.

Goodbye

I slowly get up from the floor grunting in pain; I run to my brother's side.

"Stay with me now please I can't lose you," I cry out holding my brother in my arms.

"It's okay just promise me that you'll get this guy for me and kill him," he said struggling to breathe for air.

"Of course," I said with tears rolling down my cheeks.

"You know I hate it when you cry, I think you should become the Black Angel, know that I will always be in your heart. Take care of the others for me and become the brave woman I know you to be," he says as his eyes slowly close as he takes his last breath, I cry with his dying words echoing in my ears I cradle him in my arms just weeping. My older brother died in my arms, and I felt like the world was ending.

After his last breath I hear people running towards me I look up and see my brothers and father. They see me cradling Jake in my small arms I shake my head at them with tears streaming down my face and returning to face my brother to cry even more. Father drops to his knees at the sight of his eldest son's dead body and comes to my side taking me in his arms as I begin to cry harder. My brothers start to have a few tears rolling down their checks. I felt like a part of me had died with Jake, but I knew I would get justice for him.

We took his body to a hospital so that they could check my current injuries and perform an autopsy on my brother's body.

51

During the fight I had received internal bleeding and two broken bones with a bruised back if I hadn't arrived at the hospital, I probably would have joined my brother in death, but I would do anything to see him again.

On April the 1st that day was always Jake's favourite even if he was sad, it would be his favourite day. On that day we decided we would put him to rest. Many people turned up to his funeral Dad said a few words, but I really wasn't paying attention, soon it was my turn to speak, I took a deep breath and walked towards the top of the casket.

"I don't know where to start. But Jake was the best brother I could have had, I know I had left for two years for a job opportunity, and I only told him before I left, and before he died he said, 'Follow your heart and let nothing hold you back'. I wish I had spent more time with him, but he wanted me to announce this to the public and to the world; this is why I asked a few reporters here but before he died, he told me that he was working with the woman in black and he was known as Black Cub. The woman in black also asked my brother to announce to the public what you will call her. She wished to be called The Black Angel." I turn around and see a ghostlike figure of my brother that I can only see, he smiles at me, I mouth him goodbye and then he disappeared like mother had, like smoke blowing away. I could hear the reporters trying to speak to me, but I just pretend that they're not there.

After the service we had an after party gathering and I saw some of my old school friends and they paid me their respects.

"Hey Zari, long time no see," Charlie said, I hugged him; it had been over two years since I had seen him. He chuckled at my reaction to seeing him in such a long time.

"I have missed you and I am so sorry that I didn't tell you

that I was leaving for two years but I have wanted to see you since I got back, I just couldn't find you," I said after releasing him from the hug.

"I have missed you too and I forgive you and I'm sorry about your brother I wish there was something I could do but it is good to see you again. Also, who is the boy who looks exactly like Jake? I don't remember you having a third brother," he replied.

I was so glad I saw him he made me feel like my world wasn't crumbling.

"He is Jake's twin brother. During my two years away, I found him in America and those boys over there they are my friends that I met in America, and they seem to drool over me all the time," I answered his question and laughed at the last part.

"Seems like a lot of people fancy you, shame, you don't do lovey-dovey stuff like that." We laughed as he was trying to do an impression of me when I told Theo off about Charlie and I being the cutest couple.

We talked for the rest of the evening having a couple of drinks. Surprisingly, I wasn't getting drunk, it must have been from the amount I had drunk in Russia; their vodka was strong but the drink I was drinking was just normal drinks to me whereas you could tell it was affecting everyone else including my brothers.

During the night I could feel someone behind me but every time I looked there was no one there. Then I thought Jake's and Mother's ghosts must be watching. When I was alone, I thought hard about the best moments I had with them then both of them appeared before my eyes I smiled at them.

"Oh, my little girl is all grown up I am so proud of you," My mum said to me in a quiet tone.

"My little sister. Nice speech. Did you tell Dad that you are the Black Angel or the woman in black?"

"No, I thought it was best if they didn't know, I want to keep them protected like I should have with you," I said looking down.

"Zari you are the best woman I know besides Mom, but you are strong, and I gave my life to help you stay safe during fighting with Bretherstone and I knew there would be consequences and if that meant me dying but you getting closer to catching this man then I would do anything for my sister," Jake said as if he was a humble man who was at peace with anything.

"We will be with you all the way and we will not leave your side, be the hero I know you can be," my mother said with a small smile on her face before both Mother and Jake disappeared like smoke, I always thought it was an amazing sight, seeing them disappear. It was all so real that I would not have Jake fully in my life any more as a real person but as a ghost who was always by my side, I was always able to sense him near me.

I had thought about what Jake and Mother had said about protecting everyone and taking care of the rest of my family and become something more and I would always have them both by my side no matter what. I knew what I had to do. I had to become a strong and independent person and protect the city and everything I care about.

Start of a new beginning

Over the course of the following events during the last two and a half years.

- Meeting Bretherstone.
- Getting my abilities.
- Being on the run for two years.
- Finding Jax.
- Going home and protecting my family.
- Training Jake.
- Fight Bretherstone.
- Then watching my brother die right before my eyes.

All these events have been my fate and more events like these are coming in the future. But my life is going to get harder. Bretherstone is still a threat to my home and my family, but I know one day I will catch him and get justice for my brother. I am now going to be the Black Angel.

I am going to inspire people and be a hero. In memory of my brother.

Black Angel is now my future.

Part Two

A Couple Months After

It had been a couple of months since Jake's death, I still wasn't in the right mindset after he died, every time I got close to Ollie my emotions got the better of me and nearly every time I was close to catching him, I almost killed him, but I didn't. That's not what my brother would have wanted. I had a glass casing for my brother's suit and I had a mannequin for my suit. My suit was a skinny fit black top and leggings with a black leather jacket and heeled black ankle boots that stayed close to my leg. Mickie and Frankie have been helping me out by looking after the city while I was out.

I was at the bunker thinking and sorting out weapons when I heard metal fall to the floor, I instantly grabbed a knife and sneak round quietly, as close to the shadows. I only hear one set of footsteps, but I still don't leave the weapon. I creep round the corner as quickly and silently as I can I walk towards the person and grab him by the collar and place the knife dangerously close to his neck.

"You move, you get your throat cut," I say in his ear in a threatening voice.

He takes a deep breath and says, "I am not here to harm you. I understand why you have a knife to my throat, and I want to help you."

I didn't trust him, but his voice sounded genuine, I remove the knife and let go of his collar. Very slowly he turned around to look at me, he had brown eyes with black hair with a very paled skin. I recognize him but I can't think of where. He looks at me with sorrow in his eyes.

"Remember the night those chemicals that went off I was there, and I was the person who told Oliver about the people out front. I was also one of the lieutenants who you fought a couple of months ago and before you try to kill me, I want to help you," he says holding his hands up in the air.

I just froze at him but keeping an emotionless stare on him so he could read what I was thinking I didn't know whether to trust him or not, but I thought about the future. In my mind I was seeing me and him working together, and we were actually trusting each other.

"All right I guess I will let you help me but there is one thing I want to know, why did you decide to join me?" I ask breaking the stare, he looks at the floor when I say the last part.

"Your brother wasn't the only person he killed, he killed my sister, Jessie a few days after he killed your brother. Your brother and my sister were together, and he killed her because he thought she was going to help you," he said putting his hands down and tearing up a bit talking about his sister.

"So, you want to get justice for her just like I want to with my brother?" I ask him.

He nods his head.

After he offered his proposal, I decided that we would work together, I told him this and he seemed happy. I thought, *if he is now on my side, he could tell me Ollie's plan and have a little advantage against him.*

After a few hours of talking and showing him around the bunker he seemed like he knew what our common goals were and he sees my brother suit and gives me a sad smile, I just smile back.

"I met Jake once he was a really nice guy, and he was the only person I met who treated my sister right," he says out of the blue.

"I missed that, I guess, I never met your sister I didn't even know he had a girlfriend, but I would have if had never met Ollie and they would both still be alive." I blame myself looking down at the ground.

He gently places his hand on my shoulder, I flinch at his touch he sees this but doesn't remove his hand.

"It's not your fault they died, for months now Ollie has been threating to kill my sister because he could tell that I was having second thoughts and your brother died protecting you and that is what he wanted. When I first met him, I asked him did he have any siblings and he said that he had a missing twin brother, younger set of twins, brother and sister, but the sister was missing, he seemed a bit like a ghost when talking about his sister you he obviously missed you very much.

He said that he regretted a lot of things after you disappeared that was when I started to have second thoughts about Ollie," he said in a humble tone.

After the very touching moment we continued to trust each other more and we started training. He put up a good fight but was very rusty as he would have used a gun, but he had a couple of good moves. I taught him the same way I did Jake; no mercy, no breaks he took it completely different to my brother and wasn't asking he just got right back up and kept going.

Destiny

It had been a few weeks since me and Roy had formed an alliance and banded together for the same cause to defeat Bretherstone he is still headline news we had made sure that we got where he was attacking and stopped a few of his heists. Slowly a few of Bretherstone's men saw what he was doing was wrong and his numbers where decreasing. Roy kept contact with a few of his old buddies from his days with Bretherstone.

It was August the 27th a normal day, and I was doing normal training doing the punch bag for stress relief. When Roy came up to me looking like he something on his chest he was just standing there like an idiot. Trying to find the words to tell me something important but was struggling, he looked so lost.

It wasn't until I stopped punching, that he looked up and looked like he had something to spill out and was ready to.

"I hope you don't mind me having a look through those history books, but I was a bit curious about the person Ollie was talking about destiny and stuff I met the guy, he wasn't a godlike person more of a plain man," he said looking extremely nervous.

I had a sweaty face and was panting a bit my arms were aching and sore; I threw a towel over my shoulder.

"Spit it out, don't be shy," I said at him with a hard stare.

"Sorry, it was just that he was called Perseus and he called himself a god of destiny, but the three fates are the gods of destiny along with a couple of relics claimed to be tools of destiny, but they have been lost for centuries," he says quietly looking down, putting his nose into a book.

"You know there's a legend among the league 'One must travel to find the truth and find their life ahead of them'. I have been close to where the legend leads to from my travels."

We talked about the legend, and I knew where it was but no one had ever been able to find it but there was another legend 'a woman of great power will hold power like no other and will meet the great gods'. I had asked the leader of the league more about it, but he just gave me a copy of the ancient text.

We read the part about the woman of great power, the phrase 'she will be known as an angel having a traumatic past' caught my eye. Black Angel was the name I was given when I was in the league my Latin name was *Angelus ad nigrum* that means The Black Angel that's why I chose that name as I thought that it would lead me to a better future.

My past wasn't the best, my mother dying, the accident, these powers, Jake dying.

"What if you're the woman in the legend, I mean everything that it says has a link to you, here, look, 'she will have a partner who would have betrayed her enemy to fight with her' I mean I'm the partner who betrayed your enemy. And here, 'she will have power like no other human being as if she was blessed by God' you were given abilities, come on, you have to be the woman in the legend," Roy says ranting out as if all of this is all true, but a legend has to be dead, and I am not dead.

I shrugged it off, walked away from Roy and went towards the training area where I was using an array of weapons and used the target practice to see what my skills were like. Out of the corner of my eye I noticed Roy coming towards me I just kept trying out different weapons.

"We should go to that place where we think those fates are,"

Roy says after I had finished trying out all of the weapons.

"Well then if you think it's for the best then we'll go. But we are going to the league first as they most likely have more knowledge of the island as they have that island in their territory. No arguing," I say giving him a stern look, he nods.

We spend a few days packing and some final sparing lessons to make sure that we are all ready in case of emergencies and anything that might come across our path.

On September the 7th we had everything ready, I had contacted an old friend of mine called Peter Dale who had a plane that we could use and possibly borrow in return for what I had done for him.

"So how do you know this guy again?" Roy asked for the millionth time.

"I told you I met him in a Russian pub, and I helped him collect a load of items," I say in an annoyed tone.

"So, you stole things for him?" he asked in a questionable tone.

"No, I gathered people to help him by recruiting them, technically I didn't commit any type of crime not even underage drinking as in Russia you're allowed to drink from the age of twelve and above. So—" I say in a calm tone.

"You already boss?" Frankie asks.

"We'll make sure that the city and the country are safe—" Mickie says starting a sentence doing that twin thing.

"No one can stop the twin boys," Frankie says finishing his sentence and fist bumping his twin I roll my eyes at them.

"Are you sure that you want them two in charge?" Roy asks.

"You do know those two used to do boxing I think they can handle a couple of weeks without me here if anything major happens they will catch them and call out the police right boys."

I say looking at Roy then turning my head to look at the twins.

"Yeah, well you know we obey you," They say in unison; I raise an eyebrow at them, but I say bye to them with a hug and they waved us off and said good luck they knew something Roy didn't know about how we were getting there we had everything we needed. I transformed into my wolf self while Roy walked all the way to an abandoned airbase.

The Flight

We were approached by a middle-aged man with brown hair and beard he looked very scruffy with a black fur coat. I changed into my human form while Mr Dale gave a weak smile towards us.

"Once again, we met who is this you have brought with you. A lover?" he said he in a deep voice.

"Why does everyone think that, he is an acquaintance helping me in a common cause," I say back at him with anger in my voice.

"Sorry about your brother and your sister Mr Barker," he says with a saddened tone.

I thought, *how did he know about that I mean a lot of people know about my brother but how did he know about Roy's sister?* I turned to look at Roy, he had his head down at the mention of his sister.

With a little talk we bordered the small plane, Peter wasn't coming with us, but we had a pilot, the plane was so small but had enough room. There was a set of parachutes just in case we made it to the island. Roy was quiet throughout most of the journey.

"Do you have any other siblings?" I asked out of the blue, I wanted to get to know him better after all if we were going to work together, we needed to get to know each other better.

"I have my other sister Lizzy and that's it. You?" he answered.

"I only have Jax and Behrad," I answered back.

We talked for a couple of hours; overall the whole plane ride was seven hours. When we reached the island there was no landing area and I had forgot to mention that we would have to jump out of the plane to get there.

"What are you like with jumping out of plane and heights?" I asked with a faint smirk on my face. He just looked at me wide eyed as if in was an alien.

"Never jumped out of a plane all right with heights. Why?" he asked looking nervous and worried.

I laughed a little at his reaction. "Well there is no landing area, so we are going to have to jump and parachute down," I said with a plain look.

"You're serious!" he yelled out. I don't think he had ever done anything like it before. I nodded, trying to be reassuring he seemed to calm down a bit.

I attached all our things to a special parachute that would go off when it reached a certain height. I grabbed the two other sets and threw one at Roy's face suggesting for him to put it on which he did very gingerly. I buckled the straps and watch Roy to make sure he done it right which he had. Sliding open the plane door, I slung out our gear shoot and watched it reach opening height.

"Ready to jump," I said whilst walking towards the open doors with Roy at my side.

"No," he said, and I gave him a light push to push him out of the door he screamed so loudly I'm sure my eardrums blew. I also jumped out but laughing at Roy's facial expression.

When we were mid-air, I shouted to Roy to release the parachute which he did as soon as I said it, I just shook my head and released my one.

He soon was floating smoothly down to the ground and not

67

falling I saw that our things had landed on the floor we only brought a few clothes and weapons. I had a radio in my pocket to call our pilot with as soon as we ready to leave.

I landed gracefully on the ground whereas Roy didn't land too well and as soon as he had gotten back to his feet, he started puking, it seems like that didn't go to well with his lunch.

"Thanks for waiting till we landed I'm sure no one would have wanted puke to fall in their face," I say laughing at him.

"You're welcome so this is the island of the league," he says wiping his mouth.

"Yep, we just have to wait for my friend Courtney or Light," I say looking around turning my body looking in all directions.

"Light?" He says placing his hands on his knee bending over. I nod.

"it's good to see you again, *Angelus ad nigrum*," someone says behind me, I turn around to face I short young woman with black hair and eyes she smiles at me, I return the smile.

"It is good to see you to, Lux," I speak. To Roy I whisper that Lux means Light in Latin.

The League

We engulf each other in a hug forgetting about Roy we talk about things only me and Courtney would know about.

"You know I am here, Zari, and you must be Courtney," he says extending his hand to Courtney.

"You never mentioned a man that looked like one of the men who attacked us and he looks like an idiot was coming with you," Courtney says giving him grief and looking down upon him.

"He's helping me with catching the person who caused the league to be attacked, we need your help," I say looking at Roy then back at Courtney.

"Very well, follow me," She says looking at Roy then returning to face me.

She starts to lead the way with me behind and Roy following close behind me not wanting to cause trouble for what his past brought upon him.

Courtney leads us towards a temple which is over centuries old, it looks in good condition and has a similar layout to old roman buildings. We walk through the dark brown oak doors with gold ring handles. There is an alter at the end of the hallway where the leader would usually sit, many league members standing in neat rows facing us. They were all wearing black clothing covering all of their bodies except their eyes, a sword in their left pocket with a quiver of arrows and a bow.

"This is where you were for a month?" Roy whispers in my ear but I shush him signalling that we only speak when spoken

69

to.

We reach the end of the hallway with a man in a green/black cloak with his back to us clearly the leader he looked no more than fifty.

"It is good to see you again, *Angelus ad nigrum* to what do I owe this meeting," the leader asks in a deep but slightly calm voice.

"As it is to see you, Princeps," I say whilst getting down on one knee and bowing my head.

I look at Roy who isn't doing the same and he doesn't know that he is disrespecting Princeps and the whole league if he isn't careful. I nudge him in the leg with my hand he looks down at me, I signal my head telling him to do the same he quickly does the same as me.

"You may stand, what do I owe the pleasure? And why have you brought a member of your enemy along? If you wish I can torture him," he says a few moments after Roy has shown respect.

I slowly get up from the floor and so does Roy, "I am looking for the island of the gods, we seek knowledge, and he has betrayed his kind to help us," I say trying to ask for his help.

"You will have the help of my daughter, Lux as I know you to know each other you will be led to your chambers by my finest men," He says in his deep voice.

Two men come forward while the rest leave, Courtney stays by her father's side I begin to walk out when I hear the old man call me back, I walk back to the front, he signals his daughter to leave.

"I wanted to talk to you in private about the woman who has great power; as I am sure you have read the full text of the book. I wasn't sure if she was real, but she is; you are her and I am quite

70

sure that you know that too, I wanted to show you something," he says.

I nod.

He slowly turns around with his robes following him, I slowly follow him towards the chamber of Arken we walk into the room of the first leader of the league I notice a selection gold and silver relics and at the back of the room there is a glass case with many other precious items.

"Why have you brought me here?" I ask looking at him with a straight face.

He snickers a little. "The line 'the woman of great power will have blood of the first Princeps and will drink the chalice of life to give immortality to enter the island of the gods' I told you, you are the woman of great power and you are the descendant of the first Princeps," he says picking up a chalice with jewels encrusted around it and hands it to me. "Only a child of Princeps can use it, this will allow you to enter the temple without getting burned 'those without the drink of immortality will perish, those with it will be able to see the gods' true form and shall live if they enter the temple'."

I look at him with disbelief written all over my face, but I know it's true as I can see in my mind that I am, it was all crazy, but it was true.

I tell him that I am heading to my chambers he agrees I walk away, with the chalice in hand I notice that it starts to fill up with a golden liquid. I shrug it off and briskly walk towards my chambers; they are the same as my old ones, two black king size beds with red walls with torches lighting the room.

I notice Roy already asleep on one of the beds, I smile to myself and shake my head. I walk over to the other bed where my bag is, I put the chalice on my bedside table, I unzip my bag

71

and find a folded up piece of paper and I thought *I didn't pack this* I carefully unfold the piece of paper to find a load of pictures of my family and friends; there were the twins, my brothers, the guys from school, one of Roy? My parents. I feel a tear run down my cheek I slowly bring my hand up to my face when another wipes the tear away.

I look up to see Roy facing me, he sits down on the bed, I sit down next to him.

"Me, Mickie and Frankie made that for you thought you might like it and you're probably wondering why there is a picture of me in there, don't ask, Frankie put it in there so you'll have to ask him," he says sweating a little he seems to be so nervous a lot.

"Thanks, I really appreciate it just saying we are going to be staying here for a few days," I answer his nervous face he smiles and nods.

We bid each other good night, he falls asleep in his bed, and I fall into a dreamless sleep.

The next morning, I wake up really early, I change into my old league uniform, I was surprised that it still fits me. I leave Roy a note telling him to meet me in the hall of the Princeps and left him a pair of league uniforms. I walk down towards the hall of the Princeps and find no one there but I had woken up earlier than anyone in the league.

After moments of waiting, Roy and a few others walk into the room, Roy, clearly standing out, stumbles into the room.

"What exactly are we doing?" Roy asks whispering into my ears.

"Learning the way of the league and I am helping train you along with Lux and you have to call her that and not Courtney she is the daughter of the Princeps. Now stand still and stay quiet," I say in a hushed tone.

We wait for many moments for the rest of the league and Courtney. They arrive Princeps appears from the chambers of the leader.

"You all know where your places are, you may leave *Angelus ad nigrum* and Stultus you will follow my daughter," he says and walks towards his private chambers with his lieutenants.

"What does Stultus mean?" Roy asks me once everyone has left.

"Idiot," I say in pale tone.

"That's offensive," he says scrunching his face.

Courtney comes over to us and commands us to follow her to where we are going to train. We trained for hours on end my skills had become greater than Courtney's, but it took Roy hours just to be able to fight back for five minutes.

"Maybe you should try fighting my father, I mean I am the second most skilled person out of the league, and you beat me, so you have to try beating my father," Courtney says puffing from catching her breath.

"Please, he would take me down in five seconds," I say collecting a ladle of water to drink.

"Come on, you took me down in ten minutes only my father has been able to beat me," she says. "Fine. I challenge him to fight you."

I roll my eyes at her, she leaves to talk to her father while I give Roy a few private lessons.

"You're coming along, just two more days then we will go to the island. I am pretty sure that Liam will come with us, and you have to call him *tunc abel* pastor that means 'timekeeper'."

"Okay thanks for giving me a chance and I kind of want a different name."

"You have to earn it to be able to choose one," I reply to him giving him a weak smile.

We train for a few more hours, slowly improving his skills as he becomes better. When we finally finished, we are approach by the children of The Princeps (Liam and Courtney). Courtney explained that she told her father to try and fight me which Liam and her father happily agreed on.

The Challenge

"So, you want me to fight your brother and your father because—
" I ask pointing at Liam and having a confusion plastered on my face.

They were just standing there as if to say 'you have to try' but I didn't get why I had to try and fight the son of the Princeps and the Princeps.

Hesitantly I agree to go to the halls where I saw The Princeps already with a few of his best men behind him, he seemed quite stricken when his daughter was requesting him to fight me. And as equally surprised that she wanted her brother to fight me as well.

"Why is it that we are fighting? Answer me my daughter," he asked first looking at me then keeping a hard, brutal stare at his daughter.

"Father I was watching Courtney fight *Angelus ad nigrum*. Courtney was unable to beat her father that is why Courtney asked you and me to challenge her," Liam says perking up for Courtney.

"Very well, but I wish to see *Angelus ad nigrum's* skills first, my daughter, you will fight and do not take it easy on her and you will not use knifes or swords but short poles, as I do not wish for any of us to be killed or gravely injured," he says declaring what must happen, we all nod at his words.

I take off the black cloak of my uniform revealing my Black Angel suit underneath it. I smirk at the astonishment on their face as they continue to take off the cloaks to reveal lightweight clothing to fight in. I pass my cloak for Roy to take, his face is covered with worry and concern I mouth to him, 'I'll be fine' I turn back to my opponents.

Two men step towards me and Courtney, and they had a set of two different poles of metal or wood. I went for the metal ones, so did Courtney; we walked into the proper positions for a challenge which was five steps away from each other and standing sideways and face your opponent.

"When I say start you may start Lux and *Angelus ad nigrum*," he says looking between me and Courtney.

We lunge at each other, our rods collide into each other making a loud noise. Repeating over and over hitting each other she tries to hit me on the shoulders and the knees, but I am able to block her, I aim for the stomach, and the knees. She is able to block me from hitting her stomach but misses me hitting her knees. She falls down to one knee I connect my two poles as they are able to connect and make one long pole, I hit her in the face, she falls to her side as I grab her face and smash her nose into my knee. She falls to the floor unconscious.

She slowly wakes up with a bleeding nose, her brother comes over to check her out and she said that she was perfectly fine, but Liam checks her out.

The Princeps comes forward "Seems like you have proven that you could possibly take me down, only my son and I have been able to take down my daughter and now you will take down my son as your next challenge," he says once Courtney has left with a lieutenant.

"Surely she should get a time to rest because she came here straight after teaching me for seven hours and then fighting Courtney," Roy pipes up, earning himself a hard stare from the Princeps. I shush him trying to get him to stop before getting himself banished from here.

"You have great courage and I think you should earn

yourself a name, what will it be?" he says showing no emotion.

"Arrowhead, that's what I am going to be called," Roy says with a smug look on his face.

"Very well, Sagittae speculum and no, *Angelus ad nigrum* will not have a break," he says. Roy looks immensely proud of himself. *"Tunc abel* pastor get into position."

The same as Courtney did, Liam got into position facing me same way she did but with a harsh look on his face saying 'you're not going to beat me', I just smirk at him.

"You must use swords this time," he says out of the blue.

Two men come towards us with a sword in hand I pick it up with my right hand Liam does the same. We have a stare off.

"You may begin," Princeps says loudly.

He lunges straight at me swooping his swords in front of me but missing. I was blocking every hit he was aiming at me, but he was missing my attacks, I sliced a small wound on his collar bone. He was taken aback a few steps while he was fussing over the wound on his neck, I was able to take it out of his hand throw it up into the air when both mine and his swords where stuck in the chandelier. He soon saw what I had done and started to throw punches at me.

I kicked him in the face, he fell to the floor I punched him in the stomach and in the face, he lay on the floor with a bruised jaw. He was holding his face from my kicks and punches.

For the second time today the Princeps steps forward to signal the end of the fight "Seems like you have proven yourself a worthy fighter to challenge me, my daughter was right about you, that you are a brilliant fighter but I want both my daughter and son present for our fight so we will have our challenge tomorrow at dawn, be ready and I would wear the mask," he says looking at his son and daughter's bruises surrounding their faces.

Me and Roy were walking back to our room when were approached by Liam and Courtney.

"You are an absolute badass you should stay here and be a league member," Liam says with astonishment in his face.

"My skills are needed elsewhere I only came here for help and I'm in need of justice for my brother," I say looking at them with no emotion and that their offer will be declined.

"My condolences to your brother and your sister and we know that you want to get the man, but we are going with you to the island of the gods. Also, if you beat our father, you will likely be able to take the rightful place as the Princeps," Courtney says with an expression of desire as if wanting me to win against their father.

"I have no intention of becoming Princeps if I beat your dad, I will let him keep his place as the Princeps and only me and Roy are going on to that island. I only needed a map of the island so that I could have a lay of the land so," I say not wanting their father to kill me if anything happened to them.

"Fine, we'll see you tomorrow," they say and walk away.

We head back to our rooms, Roy kept bugging me about how he earned his name, I just told him to shut up every time. He said that before we fight that I was going to train with him just to stretch.

We had a league type meal which was ration food, so basic rice and beans. We went to bed to get rest but I couldn't sleep so I journeyed to the top of the temple where I would gaze upon the stars, it was always so peaceful and quiet.

"Long time no see," someone says in a quiet but calming voice behind me.

See You Again

"Saw you fighting today, being the woman I know you to be," Jake says behind me.

He walks towards me as if he was a living person and sits next to me on the ledge.

"Hey, I maybe be dead and a ghost, but I can still do normal things like sit here." He laughs at the statement.

Even as a dead man he still has a sense of humour, I bet in the afterlife he was joking around and having a laugh.

"I have missed you so much and I am getting closer to our enemy," I say with tears threating to show.

"Hey, come here." Jake sees that I am about to break down. "Just saying that I was allowed to bend the rules a little so that I could do a few things."

Jake gave me a side hug with his arm wrapped around my shoulder, I rested my head on his shoulder. We just sat there for ages looking at the stars; he talked to me about millions of things, I just sat there listening to his voice, it made me feel calm.

"I got to know mom in the afterlife, she is so kind and I think of all of us together including my twin, all the things we have missed out on by being separated all the family together time we could have had. How you have been living this life as an outcast for three years I don't know, but you are one spectacular woman, everyone is so proud," he continues talking about what has happening to him over the last couple of months.

"I just learned to always think about those you love, I always thought about you. You were always my big brother, and no one can replace you," I say slowly closing my eyes.

I sit there for a while longer with him and there in that moment I felt like I was on cloud nine; I may have Behrad and Jax but there was never going to be another Jake.

I slowly begin to fall asleep happy with the past few moments that had happened.

But I wasn't the one who had brought Jake, maybe he came here via someone else or maybe he came here out of choice because he missed me.

Princeps

The next morning, I woke up in my bed I thought *Jake must have brought me here* I look over to find Roy not in his bed.

"Morning." I look over to see Roy absolutely beaming.

"What happened to you?" I say looking at a completely happy Roy which I had never seen before.

"My sister! She came to me just the same as your brother," he says coming over to sit on my bed.

He explains about how his sister just appeared to him, and they talked for hours on end then that Jake had come into the room carrying a sleeping me. When he came, Jessie said, "It's time for us to go, bye big brother, just saying, she's a keeper."

After we explained to each other what we did when our siblings came to see us, we got ready. I didn't get into league uniform but got into my suit whereas Roy was in league uniform.

We trained in the area that we trained at the day before; his skills were improving immensely and he was starting to be able to fight back for longer and I wasn't going easy on him. So that showed me something.

It was coming near dawn, we nodded at each other and walked towards the halls where I would be fighting the Princeps in a few short moments.

"It seems like you didn't back out on the challenge but even if it wasn't a challenge, I would have asked you to try and fight me to see if your skills have improved from when I last taught you," Princeps says, taking off his cloak to reveal a small light

81

suit.

"What are we fighting with?" I asked, not moving.

"He smirks at my question. "With our bare hands, you have fought with metal poles and swords and now we will fight with our hands."

We got into position within the large fighting cage and when we walked around facing each other, we were exactly opposite each other. After a few loops were reached our original positions, we walked towards each other face to face. He started punching me in the stomach, but I made sure that he didn't touch me. While he was busy trying to hit me, I climbed up the side of the cage to the top ledge so that I could throw myself down and punch him straight in the face.

Exactly as I wanted, he fell to his knees. I kept throwing punches at him, he kept trying to hit me but missed. I didn't realise that he had gotten a small blade out and stabbed me in the left side of my stomach I take a few steps back he smirked maliciously.

"Seems like you underestimated me," he said, slowly getting up.

"I thought you said no weapons," I say holding my side to keep pressure on the wound so that it won't bleed out.

"I said using your bare hands I said nothing about any weapons."

With those words said and me being quite annoyed that he didn't make the rules clear enough but that was one of his techniques getting inside your head, so I tried blocking everything out.

I started throwing my punches at him; slowly he seemed to be weakening I was able to snatch the knife out of his hands and throw it out of the cage. After that I continue to throw punches at his face, I slowly begin to make him fall to the ground, I get my arm around his neck, slowly making him black out after a few long moments. I check for a pulse. There still was a pulse.

"Seems that you are clearly the better fighter than my father, take him to his chambers notify him that he still is the Princeps," Liam says once I have stepped out of the cage.

I look at the brother and sister and nod at them; slowly I make my way over to Roy. I look at him, he has worry filled in his eyes. I avert my eyes towards the wound on my stomach I see blood slowly flowing out of it.

"We should head to our room, I think I need rest," I say to him in a weakened voice.

He nodded, we walked down the walls that went on for what seemed like miles; we made it to our room I took off my jacket.

"You should get some rest if you want, I could have a look at the wound," Roy says changing out of the league uniform.

"When did you learn to patch up wounds and all the medical stuff?" I ask him.

"My mum was a field surgeon, and my dad was a doctor," he speaks.

He orders me to get some rest. After he brutally but calmly told me to get rest I walk to my bed to try and have a few hours' sleep while he patches up my wound.

I woke up a while later, I saw a hand holding mine I looked up and saw Roy half asleep and half-awake. I gently move my hand away from his and slowly get up, even with Roy's protests to stay still as he become fully awake, I didn't listen to him. I decided I would change my clothes Roy turned around but looked for a split second and saw scars upon scars painted on my back, he looked at me with disbelief, but I just gave him a weak smile.

Leaving

We were grabbing a few last-minute items before we were going to sail off to the island of the gods.

With everything packed, I decided that I would give Roy a gift that I had been working on for a couple of months in preparation for him becoming Arrowhead, which I knew from the moment he became a part of my crew/team.

I had made him a dark-red suit with black stitches that you could see and a detachable hood. I also bought him a quiver and bow from the same company that Jax had used to learn how to do archery. It obviously had a red mask. I thought it quite fit his personality.

Reaching down into the crate which had landed on the beach when we arrived, I opened it to find a few things and a briefcase. Slowly, I opened up the case to find the suit and everything I had ready for Roy. If he was going to be a part of my team, he was going to need a suit.

I closed the case before walking away from the crate and towards my room for one last time before heading to the boat. Walking into the room, I found Roy packing a few things.

I crept up behind him, silently I tapped him on the shoulder, he jumped when I tapped him on the shoulder. He had his hand to his chest trying to catch his breath after his little fright.

"Sorry," I say, he turns around slowly looking at me questionably.

"I have a little something for you and you're going to need

it and it shows that you are now a part if my team," I say handing him the briefcase.

He looks at it with his eyebrows furrowed, I just nod my head at him to open the case, he gives me a look before looking down at the case. Slowly undoing the locks and opening it up. He pulls out the jacket then puts it back, then placing the mask in his hands, twitching his eyes between me and the mask.

"You've earned your name, so you have earned your suit and mask you are a part of my team," I said to him with a proud look on my face.

His face was shining with happiness. He put the case down on the bed and grabs me into a very tight hug such that I almost lost my breath. He was so happy, and he was just like a kid on Christmas morning.

We changed into our suits and we decided not to have the masks on. Roy kept his hood up though. We walked off to the docks where we were met by Princeps.

"I thought I would watch you leave on your adventure and we wish you luck. By the way, like the new suit Mr Barker and we will meet again, Ms Kingston. Good luck on your journey."

We said our farewells and got into the boat starting to sail into the endless sea. I knew roughly where the island was. I pulled out the map for us to follow to reach the island.

It was a two-day sail and I had the cup in my bag of which I had to drink in order to enter the temple. We sailed and sailed we had enough ration food for us to last a week, although I didn't eat anything. I only had things to drink as I learned that the human body could last a month without eating so I was giving Roy my rations.

By the end of the second day, I could see land and a rather large temple the size of five football pitches and as tall as three double-decker buses. It was so spectacular.

However, as we were getting closer to the island, I could see a couple of other boats. I thought Ollie must be here. I looked over my shoulder and saw Roy fast asleep. Slowly I walked towards him and tapped his face. He stirred a little and opened his eyes droopily.

"Morning sleepy head," I said with a small smirk on my face.

He slowly got up from his sleeping position, stretched and got prepared. His eyes widened like saucers when he saw the boat at shore and I was quite sure that he didn't need anyone telling him that our enemy was at the place we were hoping to go.

The Island

Once we arrived on shore, we tied a rope to a wooden pole that was by the small dock area so that the boat wouldn't float away. Roy first went on to the docks then offered his hand to me to help me out of the boat, but I ignored it and got out on my own.

We walked down the five-mile track to a mountain, which wasn't that high, that we had to climb before we could get to the temple.

Roy got out his quiver and bow; I looked at him with no clue what was happening. He shot an arrow to the top of the mountain, the arrow had rope attached to the arrow.

"Hold on to me," he said, once again I ignored him and asked for the bow, I shot another arrow; we used the rope to help us up the mountain.

When we reached the top, Roy looked like he was about to die after doing a hundred-mile run, and I was the complete opposite.

Slowly he got up from sitting down, it wasn't much further to go before we were at the temple. As we were walking, Roy started talking about what he would do once all of this was over, I didn't listen to him but focused on the matter at hand.

We had reached near the barriers of the temple, when I would have to go on my own, while Roy waited but I put my hand up in a fist signalling to Roy that something was up, I could hear rustling in the bushes.

Soon enough we were surrounded by twenty or so men, they

all had guns pointing in our direction both of us knew that if we made a move, we would be dead.

"Oh, how the mighty have fallen. I have finally found my two, favourite people, uh, did you miss me?" Ollie said with a psychopathic look on his face moving towards us. He was wearing a black suit quite loosely with the two top buttons undone and no tie.

"Shut up you psycho man! We actually quite enjoyed peace and quiet without you terrorizing the city," I say spitting in his face.

He chuckles. "Aren't you the charmer?"

I slowly get a knife in my hand and pass one to Roy without anyone noticing I threw one to a person, it hit them right in the heart. I pulled out my metal rods.

"You just don't know when to quit do you?" he says, anger showing through his eyes.

The Challenges

I smirked at his remark, just in that moment we had our weapons ready and some of Ollie's men came towards us but not in the fashion I thought they would. They came and stood by our side as if they were rebelling against Ollie and joining us. Roy looked at them, they smiled at him they were obviously close with him and wanted vengeance for whatever Ollie did to them.

All of us were prepared and had our weapons out and soon enough men were coming our way this time the odds were better fifty-fifty. Ollie was standing to the side watching us like a mentor training his students.

With the shift in allegiance of some of Ollie's men, the fighting began, not always easy for us to determine who was on who's side at some points. I was hitting those still faithful him in the stomach and using my metal rods to ultimately reach the enemy. I must have taken down six men before I reached my target. He gave me a savage smile and he gently pulled out a sword from a case on his left side. The blade was perfectly sharpened and clean like it was fresh from the blacksmith. It was the same blade that was run through my brother's heart.

I pulled out my sword and without him noticing, I also pulled out a small blade that was unnoticeable; we started fighting, I was trying to remove his sword from his grasp while he was trying to take me off my feet. Our blades clashed with one another. We stood a good few steps away from each other, the knife in my left hand and the sword in my right hand. We ran towards each other and I stabbed him with the knife in his right side. When we were at opposite ends of each other, he saw that I had stabbed him shock evident on his face for a split second.

He looked at me. "You may have won the battle, but you haven't won the war." With that he disappeared through the bushes into the shadows.

I ran back to the men fighting, I saw that Roy and my new guys were struggling so I started taking down the forces and giving way for my guys to fight back. We were fighting back; when the men we were fighting saw their numbers were decreasing, they retreated disappearing through the bushes and into the shadows.

Soon we were left with dead bodies and ourselves, some were the people who joined me the rest were Ollie's guys. Blood was everywhere. Some of bodies had their eyes open. I walked to each body and closed their eyes saying, "*Ave atque vale.*" It means 'hail and farewell'.

Once I had been to everybody I walked over to the guys. They looked at me.

"Thank you for helping me, if there is anything I can do—"

"No, you don't have to do anything for us we want Bretherstone caught and thanks for letting us fight with you." So many questions swam in my mind, but the main one being why the sudden change of heart? Answers I wasn't going to get for they were already preparing to leave.

We said our farewells and they left, me and Roy looked at each other, we were alone again, I took in an awkward breath, I turned and walked towards the barrier.

It looked like a series of tests we had to complete.

There was a wheel with a little marble, I guessed I had to get the marble out. Slowly I turned the wheel. I was almost able to get it out. It took a few tries, Once I had finally gotten the marble out of the maze, the door opened. I signalled to Roy to follow me through the door.

The first task was complete.

I walked through to find a sand pit surrounded by stone slabs. I thought that the sand was quicksand and I needed away to get across. I knelt down and I saw that in the centre of the sand pit, it was raised a little. I stood back up and slowly stepped off the stone slabs onto the raised sand, I was relieved when I didn't start sinking. I held out my arms to help provide balance, it was like walking on the balance beam from gym class, but with no safety matts. My steps were slow and short I made my way across the sand, Roy followed close behind.

We had completed the second task.

The third task had different slabs with Latin words. I put a small object on a random slab, and it fell right through to the floor to a snake pit; whoever was running this place really didn't want anyone going here, the phrase *requiem animabus vestris licet, dimissis omnibus peccatis vestris, ave atque vale* was engraved on the slabs, which means 'may your souls rest, your sins forgiven, hail and farewell'. I stepped on the words of the phrase one by one, Roy followed behind making sure he didn't go on the wrong ones.

We made it to the other edge of the puzzle. The third task was complete.

"What does it mean?" Roy asked once he had come off the final slab.

"What the phrase *'requiem animabus vestris licet, dimissis omnibus peccatis vestris, ave atque vale'*," I said fluently.

He nodded.

"It means 'may your souls rest, your sins forgiven, hail and

91

farewell'."

We continued on to the fourth task; there was a series of switches on the floor which probably sets something off. We began to make our way through when Roy stepped on one, we got down just in time before we were scorched. We continued making our way through, it was like a mine field.

We made it. The fourth task was complete.

We walked through the tunnels when we came across an empty archway, it seemed too easy, I held Roy back as I stuck my hand out and put it through the archway when my arm started to burn, I yelped in pain and pulled my arm away. I held it close.

"Here, wrap this around it." He handed me a piece of cloth.

My arm was soon covered I had a light-bulb moment I scrambled to get the cup that Princeps gave me. I saw that liquid was still in the cup, the words, 'only the first Princeps descendants can enter' rang in my head.

"Wait here," I told him and took a small slurp from the cup and once again tried to walk through the archway, this time I didn't get burned.

I looked back and saw Roy standing there. "Stay there if you come through you will die."

He nodded, I turned back around and started walking down another hallway.

The Gods

I walked down the hallway and found a large room with three stone chairs; there was no one sitting there. The room was vast and wide, it was as big as an actual church but there were no beautiful stained-glass windows it was like a blank canvas.

Looking at the chairs, I noticed a word on each chair 'Lachesis' 'Clotho' and 'Atropos', the three fates. I continued to look around and saw a few small pillars that had a couple of relics on them, the relics of destiny.

"I finally get to meet you Zari Kingston," a woman says behind me, giving me a fright.

I turned around to find a middle-aged African American lady with blue Greek clothing. She was sitting in the middle chair that said 'Clotho'.

"I was wondering when I would finally meet you; your future, present and past is quite intriguing, but I imagine you have many questions."

What did she mean by that? My life was intriguing? And how did she know that I was coming?

"A man named Ollie Bretherstone was approached by someone who called himself the god of destiny," I say kneeling to show a sign of respect.

"You may stand. I know of the man who approached Mr Bretherstone, he is a messenger who seeks power using something that I want you to have and destroy. When the time comes do not tell anyone about it and do not let anyone have it. I am trusting you with a very powerful relic," she speaks.

She gets out of her chair and swiftly walks towards a bag and then towards me. I get the sense that I have to guard it with my life. Once the bag is in my hands, she disappears, and I am left alone with the bag in hand.

I walk back down the hallway, but everything seems different, soon I am back to find Roy slumped down the wall looking dehydrated, when he saw me walking back through the archway, he his eyes lit up.

"Thank god you're back," he said rushing towards me, hugging me like his life depended on it

"What do you mean I was only in there for three minutes," I say laughing, as much time couldn't have gone past.

"You've been in there for three days, I thought something had happened to you and I couldn't help you otherwise I would die just trying to get to you," he says, stuttering.

"Roy, shut up! I'm fine let's go get home and have some good sleep with no fighting or anything, just relaxing," I say demandingly.

He agrees and we slowly walk back to the boat to grab the radio so that we could contact the pilot. He said that we would have to wait a few hours. So, me and Roy sat on the beach waiting for him, we both a had a short amount of time to sleep.

We wake up just as the small flying boat plane had landed, we got into the plane, it was going to be a few more hours before we arrived home and actually have time to ourselves to rest and recharge a little.

Roy looked like he hadn't slept in ages. I guess since I was with the gods for three days, when I thought I was only going to be there for a few minutes, he was worried sick, but it was minutes for me but days for him. He had another sleep in the plane while we were flying.

I decided to have a look in the bag Clotho gave me. I pulled out a large book that has a leather case the pages were slightly loose and not in a line. Slowly I open the book and I see everything; the past the present and the future, everything that has happened and was going to happen. I quickly shut the book before I got too deep into it. Frustratingly this book with its ragged, uneven pages, just proved the greater beings were setting events in motion and had been for some time. Plotting the course of destiny.

Ultimately Clotho was right about the book though, it was dangerous, imagine if someone used it for their own personal use and changed everything and it had to be destroyed. This thing I was trusted with was immensely powerful. I had to make sure it didn't fall into the wrong hands.

Home

We landed back from where we began on this journey. Roy stirred from his slumber slowly, we walked back to the base but soon Roy looked like he was going to fall off his feet, so I transformed into my wolf form with Roy draped over my back. He was heavy but I was able to walk at an awfully slow pace for a few miles.

Soon we arrived at the edge of base camp, I dropped Roy on the ground and licked the side of his face. He woke up again and got up onto his feet. I transformed back into my human form, and we walked into the base.

When we walked in, the air didn't feel right like something was up, I couldn't hear Frankie and Mickie cheering our return I didn't hear them at all, so I placed my bags on the floor and shouted for the twins.

Soon they came out of their hiding spaces with extremely glum looks on their faces. What had happened in the couple of weeks we had been gone; what had happened that was so drastic? I looked at them with confusion. Roy, however, yawned and went upstairs to sleep. Though I wanted to know what had happened.

"Zari, I-I am so sorry." Frankie kept stuttering and was looking down at the ground muttering something that I couldn't here.

"What happened while we were gone?"

They didn't answer.

"Answer me! What in the world happened to make the most cheerful people I know to be as glum as this? So answer me!

What happened?"

They looked at me. Finally, Mickie answered me, "Zari something happened to your dad I'm so sorry we tried so hard."

I looked at them with worry, "What happened to my father?"

They took in a husky breath. "Your dad was killed I'm so sorry we tried everything we could to save him."

I just started to tear up. "It's not your fault," I say just before I start crying. I had already lost my brother not that long ago but now my father was gone too.

Part Three

Pain

Every day of the past month I had been sitting in the same spot barely eating or drinking. By the time it had come to my father's funeral, I wore a plain black outfit, I was in bad shape. I was as skinny as a paint brush. Many words were said about my father, it hasn't even been six months since Jake died, my family were being broken down piece by piece.

"My father wasn't always the best, but I had many secrets from him, I was trying to protect him. I had left him and my brothers for a little while and then he was gone. I remember that when I came back after I had been gone for two years, we got involved in an attacking. I protected my family and I ended up in hospital and all my father wanted to do was protect his little girl; he always wanted me and my brothers to be safe. He was always the man my mother wanted him to be. Even after she died," I said at the funeral.

This was just a funeral for all the people who didn't know that my family were half creatures. This funeral was for the normal people in town, his casket was filled with his favourite items. His real funeral was the other day. We met up with father's old friends. We congregated at the lake where the families would meet up. There were more of us than you think we had quite the community. When a half wolf died, we would go down to the lake put their body into a boat and they would be burned on the lake by either their eldest child or their wife/husband. Father lit my mother's. I lit Jake's. Jax lit father's.

After the service was finished, I left without any hesitation I didn't want to be around people any more if my life was just going to keep crumbling, I walked down the dark alleyways back to the base where I found my usual spot for the past month. I would sit there, tears in my eyes, my hands intertwined with my chin resting on my hands.

I was alone for a few hours until the others came back, I could hear them talking faintly about me and my mental well-being and where I was.

"You know I can hear you even when you're quiet, so don't try to be silent," I said to them in a calm tone turning towards them.

"Oh, Z, there you are we've been worried about you," Roy replied.

"You okay?" Mickie said.

"Yeah, I'm fine," I say, turning back to looking at the floor.

"No, you are not fine. You have barely eaten, slept, or even let alone had a drink you're not giving yourself a break you are killing yourself, have you thought about Jax and Behrad? They need you; they've lost you once, they can't lose you again. They have already lost so much; your mom, Jake and your dad, they don't need to lose their sister as well," Frankie bellowed as if he knew everything, I was beyond annoyed with him, when all he was doing was trying to get me back to my normal self, but I couldn't.

"Frankie either you let me grieve or you watch me take the other road in life and stop caring about anyone and anything. I want to go back to normal, but you don't know what it is like to feel pain, you don't know what it is like being me, having these abilities; you didn't even bother to call me when my father died you could have called me to come back but what did you do? You

102

did nothing. I suggest all of you should leave and you know what I'm going to do. I need a break from all of this. I need time guys; I'll see you in a while I'm going out," I say trying to get them to understand what it was like for me, it was mainly directed at Frankie so that he understood how I was feeling.

They all stared at me in shock if they want me back, they had to give me time to myself. I knew that I hadn't been myself, but I needed time. I was suffering on the inside and there was two people who could help me, but I would have to talk to each of them separately. I just hope I'll be able to find them.

After my brother's funeral I had kept in touch with the guys from school, but they didn't know that I was a vigilante, and it was probably for the best, as I didn't need more pain and suffering in my life. We had regular meet ups and not surprising, but Charlie got a couple of scholarships. We talked about our lives and how they were screwed up and both Cody's had gotten married, Charlie was engaged, Lennon had found himself a lovely girl who treated him with respect and didn't make fun of him. Theo finally asked Thea Nightheart to go out with him, and we were all like 'for god's sake you should have asked her out years ago', it was funny because he was quite embarrassed, and Thea was just laughing.

Me and Charlie had kept in good contact, we were like the friends that would always be there for each other; his fiancé came to like me over time as she didn't like Charlie hanging out with me to begin with but soon, she learned that I would never take him away from her. I wouldn't take away someone's happiness if anything I would give up my happiness for them.

I left the building in my denim jacket and plain jeans with a simple white top and my trademark black boots. It was about ten miles to get to Charlie's place, so I transformed into my wolf

103

form and ran through the woods and the back passageways. It would have taken me about two and a half hours if I had walked but in wolf form it would only take twenty minutes.

I was halfway through the woods when I picked up another wolf scent, it was musky, gunpowder and gloss I hadn't smelled it before, but I had, it was so weird, I had smelled a similar scent but never seen them before.

I was in a small area that was empty so I transformed I looked around I could smell his scent getting closer and circling me, it was rouge wolf alone looking for a pack, I could smell blood, his pack must have been attacked.

"Show yourself I can smell you and I know you can smell me, and I am not here to harm you."

I put my hands up in the air so he could see I wasn't a threat to him.

Soon enough he lunged at me in wolf form I changed into my form we were trying to bite at each other's neck and trying to get each other down. Eventually he surrendered, we were a couple of metres apart and he soon transformed into a tall figure with small features. His shirt was ripped, he had blood on the side of his face and on the left side of his stomach, he rested against a tree he was panting in pain.

I walked over to him he was a good six-foot-tall he looked familiar; he had pale-blue eyes and slightly tanned skin, but I couldn't think of where I knew him from. I tried to help him, but he kept shoving me away.

"If you let me near you, I can actually help those wounds of yours, so stop pouting like a puppy."

He let me near him where I made him sit on the ground while I sorted out his wounds, he looked at me with every ounce of energy he had.

"You should stop staring your eyes might pop out, take a picture it lasts longer," I say making eye contact.

"Sorry I just got attacked by a psycho and I'm a bit pissed as I need to get home to my siblings," he says pained whenever I touch his wounds. Once I was done, I sat next to him on the leaves that painted the ground.

"Who are you, where do you live and who are your siblings?" I say in a demanding tone clearly indicating I wanted answers and he was being very arrogant.

"My name is Vinnie Lance. I live in maple town that's in Manchester. My siblings are Kyle and Laurel Lance and I need to stop Tommy Jakes," he speaks. I wonder who Tommy is. As in, the Tommy I know.

"Wait, you know Tommy and why do you need to stop him?" I say confused.

"He is dating my sister and you know the big brother talk 'if you hurt her, I'll hurt you'," He says, laughing.

I nod at that statement.

"Anyway, now you know who I am, why don't you tell me who you are."

"My name is Zari Kingston. I live in Liverpool about five miles away from here. I have three brothers, one's dead and both my parents are dead, and my friends want me to turn back to normal," I say ranting about my problems.

"Seems like you're having a bad day too, follow me I know a place where all your problems wash away." He slowly got up and offered me his hand I looked at it with concern but he gave me a reassuring smile, and so I took his hand.

We walked through the woods towards a small village where there was an abandoned clock tower, we walked up the flights of stairs soon we were at the top of the building. Vinnie let go of my

105

hand and walked towards a draped sheet where he grinned at me before pulling the sheet back showing the sunset and the village; Vinnie was right, your problems wash away with this view.

It was beautiful, the sunset colours glaring across the village, the sun highlighting the buildings' shape, it was amazing, I couldn't believe what I was seeing.

"I used to live here as a kid before my dad died and I believe that my dad and your parents were killed by the same man," he says, I look at him with confusion.

"If you think about it, you were five when your mom died, I was twelve when my dad died, and you were nineteen when your dad died, and they all died on June the 15th."

"What are you saying? I know the man who killed my parents is the same man but how do you know so much about me?"

"Me and your brother Jake were good friends, I was at both his and your dad's funeral that's where you recognize me from, I can't believe your brother was a hero and I know you're the Black Angel. That scrap we had I'm quite sure you won."

I stare at him with my fist clenched. How had I not known any of my brothers friends, there was so much that I missed out on by being away and having no contact.

"You weren't the only person who watched him die, I came here to catch our parents' killer, he said you would be able to help me. You are just as amazing in wolf form in a fight as you are in hand-to-hand combat, you're a pretty skilled fighter, your brother always said you could pack a punch and that was easily proven."

He was explaining many things about him and my brother. I was just not understanding why everyone was expecting me to be a hero and solve everyone's problems, but Vinnie told me it was okay to have problems and be saved. I got to know him as we talked. It was nice to have a normal conversation, he was like me but not six feet deep in trouble.

"Listen I have to go meet up with a friend, do you mind if you meet me at 73 Whitmore Street at the abandoned factory?" I say to him, getting up into my feet.

"Sure, I hope you have a good time with your friend, and I will see you later," he said also getting up.

We parted ways; Charlie didn't live far from where we were. Vinnie Headed off in the direction I had just come from, me I continued on my path in the opposite direction on route to Charlie's.

What is Going on?

Soon I arrived at Charlie's current house, I knocked three times on the door, and I waited patiently for the door to open. When it didn't I knocked on the door again, paying more attention I saw that it had been broken into. I slowly opened the door to reveal the place had been turned over and trashed, there was blood on the walls and it looked like someone put up a good fight.

I walked in, turning my head around letting my shifter senses come to the surface, assessing the situation, I pulled out a small pocketknife from my pocket. I kept walking through the hallway where I discovered a body beaten up and bruised. I rushed towards the body, it was Charlie's I looked over and saw his fiancé's body. Both of them had a slight pulse, I let out a husky breath that I didn't know I was holding. I looked up and started staring at the pale grey wall that had no pictures where there should be, it was like a blank canvas but now all I could see was writing in blood.

I slowly got up from my kneeling position keeping a firm grip on the knife, my bottom lip trembling slightly. There was a message 'I'm only here for you Ms Kingston I'm coming for you'. Whoever it was they had just declared war; this wasn't Bretherstone he would never hurt Charlie as he would never harm one of his first friends, they meant something to the both of us.

Coming out of my trance I dialled both an ambulance and Roy. I didn't want to, but he was the only person who could help me right now. He said he would be here as soon as he could get here. I waited for a few minutes when I heard a familiar motorcycle pull up' it was mine, the boys quite often used it as they couldn't drive luckily, I could, and they kept stealing my bike for their own use.

He ran into the house as if there was a tortoise chasing him. Eventually he arrived at the house.

"You know you're slower than a sloth, I got two people here on the brink of death and you are walking around as if it is a fine Sunday morning," I say scowling at him.

"Listen I'm sorry but you didn't exactly tell me why I am here and the only reason I came is because they told me if you ever called, I had to answer," he explains with a small serious face.

"Oh, so all of you can watch me twenty-four-seven, when I, the one who leads the team, has special abilities and what not, has to be watched like a two-year-old. Pathetic. Just help me," I say emphasising my frustration with the whole watching situation.

I head back to the house to find Charlie and Lauren (his fiancé) in the same place on the floor unconscious, almost lifeless. Roy quickly examines the extent of their injuries. Charlie has two bruised ribs and many bruised joints and a concussion from what he could tell. Lauren only has a concussion and a fractured, possibly broken wrist they are both still out of it from the blows they received.

I showed Roy the writing on the wall he was stunned he couldn't take his eyes off the wall he thought it was Bretherstone but once I had drummed it into his head that Bretherstone wouldn't do such a thing towards an old friend or at least I thought that was the case. However, we were old friends, but he started the war, he lost a couple of battles and won some so

109

neither side was winning.

We waited for the ambulance to arrive when they turned up, they said they would give me a ring when they had updates on Charlie and his fiancé's conditions.

They were put onto stretchers, carried, and carefully placed into the green and yellow vehicle and dashed off down the road towards the nearest hospital.

We left the broken and bruised building. Roy nodded towards the bike, but I refused, I was still mad at the boys, after all, I haven't been myself, but I needed this time to grieve and regroup. I stand on the front porch and watch Roy leave; I stand there for a little while until finally deciding to leave.

I slowly walk off the front porch towards the back street, I turn my head in all directions to make sure no one is watching me. Once I was sure it was all clear, I transformed into a wolf and ran home, millions of thoughts were caught up in a loop running through my mind bombarding my senses.

I was in the clearing again; my head was in pain. I stopped, transformed, and held my head trying to sooth the pain. Flashes running through my mind. Explosions. Shouting. Heartbreak. Endless flashes. I dropped to my knees still holding my head, the images come at me so fast. Then it all vanished I took in deep shallow breaths, I look around wide-eyed, I see that we only have a couple of hours left of light.

I forget all of what happened trying to recall it only caused more pain, there was still a few miles to go so I transform back and return to running. Soon I ended up back at the factory. I transformed and slowly walked back, I could hear shouting when I walked in, I saw Mickie and Vinnie bickering like a pair of two year olds.

"Hey!" I shout. It doesn't work. "Hey!" I scream at them;

they finally look at me. "What the bloody hell is going on here?" They look at me like I'm a statue. "Well answer or am I going to have to rip your throats out."

"This dude knows who you are and your h-e-r-o name," Mickie said.

"You do know that I knew her brother. Also, I was there when he died, and Zari invited me here and I can spell," Vinnie said.

After Vinnie had spoken the arguing had begun again, I shout at them again.

"Shut up the two of you or do I have to punch you," I yelled at the top of my lungs with my arms crossed, they all looked at me then quickly glanced at the floor knowing I mean business this time.

My face was red my blood was pumping furiously. They both started to explain themselves, I got quite a few apologies out of Mickie for everything I felt like I was the mother of this idiotic group. Mickie thought Vinnie was an enemy.

"Well how about we start this all over and not treat our guest as a psychopathic ferocious killing bloodhound that's going to take our heads of shall we." Mickie agreed and they reintroduced each other.

I explained why Vinnie was there and why he was going to be working with us and that we have a hunch. I told Mickie everything, what was at the house; the blood on the wall with the written message, our parents' murder specifically the ate connection.

"So, you're telling me that both your parents and your dad's death are related and that they were killed by the same man on the same day in the space of seven years," Mickie said pointing out the details, his eyebrows furrowed slightly figuring out and

111

processing every single detail.

After the long-winded explanation, we went to our respective rooms. But I couldn't sleep, my head was riddled with information, I don't why, but I thought back to Mother's death.

The Past

The day my mother died; I was with her. We would walk around the fields every Sunday morning to have mother-daughter time, it was always our special day. Dad, and the boys would have father-son time.

We were walking around when Mother's senses picked up something, she could hear something rustling behind us. She seemed worried and said something about 'he's back' under her breath. I was looking up at her, my eyes were wide my face was trembling. She turned her head around millions of times, fear was evident.

My mother crouched down holding my hands in hers.

"My beautiful daughter you remember the tree that was the one you and your brothers played hide and seek by?"

I nodded and she looked down at the ground and then back into my eyes, her face was contorted with sadden expressions.

"I need you to run as fast as you can to that place, and you don't leave that spot until either your brothers or dad comes, and you tell them everything that has just happened."

I nodded, she had small tears dropping from her eyes.

I started running but I stopped at the part where I could just see through the barley and wheat. I could faintly see my mother standing alone with a bow and arrows; I wondered how she got them, but I guessed with what she said she kept a weapon close to her to protect her. My breathing was low and short.

A group of people emerged from beneath the barley and

wheat they started talking but my mother must have made a snarky comment as they began fighting, I jumped with fright. She put up a fairly good fight but one of them caught her off guard, pulled an arrow out her quiver and plunged it into her stomach. I covered my mouth to stifle the scream to trying to escape and ran to the tree where mother told me to run.

I waited there for hours, eventually I heard shouting calling for me and mother. Soon father found me.

"Zari, oh, thank God you're okay," he said, slowly picking me up into his arms and carrying me back to the house.

He gently placed my small body on a chair. Covering me in a large blanket, my skin was as pale as snow, the heat of my breath was ice cold. My father went back outside to find Mother whilst Jake and Behrad stayed with me to keep me company as I had been alone for hours in the cold waiting for someone to find me.

Eventually both of my brothers fell asleep from the lack of sugar as we needed to take in double the amount a normal human should. I needed to sleep but I wanted to wait for Father. Soon he came back with a few friends, blank expressions on all their faces and something wrapped up at the time I wasn't sure what it was but now I know that it was Mother's body. They talked about something for a few hours, their voices almost inaudible, but I could hear a few words.

"He's coming."

"You need to run."

"The lances are off-grid, no one knows where they are."

"Kingston's, Lance's, Peacock's, Pearce's, Allen's."

"At least one parent from each family have died on June the 15th."

"Not the Lances."

114

"Sara Kingston, Jonathan Peacock, Harry Pearce and Mary Allen."

"Lucy (Peacock), you, Jack and Paula (Lance), Lily (Pearce) and Michael (Allen) need to stay protected from him he's coming."

"You lot defeated him once you won't be able to next time, not with most of you being dead."

"But haven't you heard the legend?"

"The legend about those five kids?"

"An angel, an archer, a lone wolf, half twins and his own blood will defeat the evil."

I was able to hear those words before they came into the room and bid goodbye to Father. After they left, I don't know what happened next as I fell into a deep slumber.

The next morning, we awoke to Father getting us ready for Mum's funeral. We wore simple clothing but we each had a lily in our hands ready to put in the lake.

The lake was the size of three football pitches. It was beautiful and peaceful at the lake, Mum used to take me and brothers there to talk about our heritage and look at the beauty of nature.

Mother and Father came here when three of their friends died, we weren't allowed to come, only when Mum died, the same with the other children. The children could only come if it was their parent who died.

People from the families that were spoken of were there, even the Lances, all of them, I guess it's where I met Vinnie for the first time.

Me, Father, Jake and Behrad walked slowly to the boat, we looked down, we saw Mum's body wrapped in a pale-cream cloth using black rope to keep it together. My brothers' eyes were glistening in the sun; I could feel small drops of water running down my face. My father sent us to stand with the Lances while him, Jack (Lance), Michael (Allen) along with father's best friend, David made the final preparation for the ceremony.

They slowly pushed the boat into the lake. Once it was floating on the lake and swaying away, Father picked up Mum's bow and arrows lighting one of the arrows and shooting it right in the centre of the boat lighting it completely on fire.

We watched the boat burn until there was nothing left. Father talked to his mates. Jake and Behrad played with Vinnie and Kyle; Laurel was only a baby. I sat at the edge of the lake where me and Mum would watch the sunset. But I remembered something Mum showed me; a treasure site on the edge of the lake where her and her sister (Annie) buried valuable items.

I stealthily walked to the smoke shack where I grabbed a shovel. I kept turning my head making sure no one was following me. I walked away from the crowd to a secluded area; Mum and Annie used to play here.

Mum said they buried the box near a willow tree to the north. I saw a tree that had the symbol of our pack. Everyone who came to my mother's funeral had it including children it was like a birth mark. I caught a glimpse of a black marking on the tree. The symbol was Celtic or Egyptian. It was two xs with a line down the centre of each, two edges were connected. A little spiral came out on the other end of the xs. There was a dot in the middle of the connected lines. I saw it was the symbol of the pack. I started to dig.

I suddenly hit something other than dirt, I drop down to my knees and use my hands to remove the dirt. Once all the dirt is removed, I see a metal box, I pick it up, but I hear someone behind me. I turn to look, and I see another wolf who looked just like Mum, pure white but black ears and feet.

She transforms into a young lady about early thirties, simple complexion. She was so similar to my mum. It was Auntie Annie.

"Who is my favourite niece," she said, crouching down and engulfing me in a hug.

"Auntie Annie, I'm your only niece." We both chuckled at my comment.

"I see that you found mine and your mother's trinket box. What are you doing out here all on your own? Is it because you have no one to talk to?"

I nod.

"Well, shall we go back before your father worries; he's lost another person in his life."

I nod.

She slowly stands up holding out her hand, I take it and grab the box with my other hand we talked about a lot of things on our walk back, it was just like being with my mum, I couldn't help thinking that I was replacing her with Auntie Annie, but I think she was just trying to lift my spirts.

We arrived back at the gathering where Auntie Annie took me towards Father's group of friends. Him and Annie had a laugh while I went back to my brothers; it was dark by the time we got home.

To this day I still have the box but have never opened it. I have never told anyone that I saw my mother die. Even my father didn't know but I guess that was because I didn't want him running off into a wild goose chase.

New Threat

Once I had played the past memories in my mind, I crept downstairs slowly and as silently as possible. I had to write down everything I heard the night of my mother's death:

- The names of the families that were mentioned.
- Who had died: Jack Lance, Sara, and Jimmy Kingston, Jonathan and Lucy Peacock, Harry Pearce, and Mary Allen.
- The date: June the 15th.
- The years: 1980, 1981, 1982, 1985, 1992, 1998, 1999.
- An angel, an archer, a lone wolf, half twins and his own blood will defeat the evil.
- Those left alive: Paula Lance, Lily Pearce, and Michael Allen.

What did they mean by 'An angel, an archer, a lone wolf, half twins, defeat the evil'? I had been working on the links between them. How were they killed? What they were up against? I needed help from something who had a large role to play in this evil that was coming.

By the time I was finished a whole board was covered in information, it was clearer now that I was onto something instead of swirling around my head. I wasn't sure what the time was but I'm sure it was now the morning, as I could heard slow footsteps. When I turned around to look at the boys, they all slumped groggily they all had messed up hair and bags under their eyes.

"Good morning campers, sleep well or did we decide to go

118

out to a night club and come back at early hours of the morning? Am I right?" I said to them with a smirk on my face looking at them, by the sound of my tone towards them, I'm quite sure they knew that they were in trouble.

"You heard us," they all looked at me wide-eyed, mouths open.

"Well, I hope that the expression on my face teaches you a lesson as well as your hangovers. Well, while you lot were pissing around being idiots, I was doing something productive. Now why don't you all get yourselves looking presentable," I said with a large smirk on my face, they immediately obeyed my words.

While they made themselves presentable, I went through the latest of the wolf news. I tried to go back to what my father and his friends were talking about that night, but so far just going through a small amount of the files, there was no mention of anything that would relate to the families not even their deaths or how they happened, only that they died.

For three days I had been going through the archives of the wolf news for the past thirty years, but nothing came up. Nothing. Not even a thing to say why the Lances went off-grid. Nothing to say that my mother was killed by a bunch of guys. It was like it never existed.

"Maybe you need to speak to someone who was involved who is alive," Vinnie said. After a three-day long search through the archives, we had gone through the whole archives twice and both times, we found nothing. "Wait, I thought you could talk to the dead."

"I can but I can only talk to them if they come to me so it's a little hard, I can't call them at will and it's hard to raise them from the dead if their spirits don't want to come back to life," I say in a tone that proved that I was bored and exhausted.

"So no seeing my dad?" he asks with slight tears in his eyes. I shake my head turning my head away.

But then I thought we could ask the remaining people alive. I looked at the board on the wall and saw that there was only three of them left alive of what we know so far. I still had an address for each of them.

Vinnie thought the same thing, we both agreed that we need to speak to someone who was involved in the thing my father was talking about the night my mother died.

On October the 5th 1999. We first visited Michael Allen he lived at:

32 Mikaelson street.

It was an hour from our base. Me and Vinnie went down the oak trail which linked the friends together it was the reason my family were a lone pack because it was easier to protect each other but my father stayed in touch with the others.

We travelled in wolf form, I couldn't help but catch a glimpse of Vinnie staring at me then when I look at him, he instantly turns his head. Why is it that guys always find me attractive? First Charlie, then the twins, Roy and now Vinnie.

I try my best to ignore Vinnie's stares. We eventually arrive at Mr Allen's bungalow; we would have arrived quicker if it hadn't had been for Vinnie's dawdle on the way here. If we had run here, we would have been here a good thirty minutes earlier.

We had a quick look around the premises. Vinnie looked round back whilst I looked around front, I saw the door was slightly open, it had wood near the handle; the wood was uneven. I slowly knelt down so that I could grab the knife that was attached to my leg. I held in my hand the sharp edge facing behind me in my left hand. I opened the door and had a look around, the kitchen and the hallway were clear. The bedrooms were clear. The living room was at the back of the bungalow. We were too late Mr Allen was dead and he had no wounds.

However, there was writing on the wall. 'His death was not my doing but I am coming for you'. Vinnie walked through the same way I did. He saw the writing and Mr Allen's body. I shook my head. Frustration bubbling inside me that possible answers were so close, but snatched away yet again.

I ran back to the base while Vinnie got people in to take Mr Allen's body, he said he would be back in a few hours. I wrote more on my board of information; the twins came back they had visited Lily Pearce she had a quite a bit of information to share.

"Mrs Pearce said that the guy's name was Klaus; one of the most powerful wolves and one of the most feared of all time. Apparently, he found a way to become ageless, he has been around for three hundred years. She said that they fought him back in 1972. He swore revenge on the families that he would return and kill them when they were least expecting it and had become settled in their lives. She said that he was going to try and prevent the legend. Apparently, his power was taken away in 1972 and slowly his power is coming back," Mickie said whilst Frankie was too busy looking for something.

We stood still waiting for Frankie to explain what exactly he was doing, he was flipping through numerous books many from the archives but some from the league. He didn't know Latin, but he knew what he was looking for. He finally found what he was looking for, his face showed pure delight that he found what he was looking for. He placed the book of legends on the table, the page was about a man.

"I don't know Latin, but I know that's about Klaus, she spoke some words in Latin, '*quartus mense in die plenæ lunæ*

121

reversurus est in Novo millennio ineunte de he is erit ad plenam fortitudinem',"

"It means 'in the new millennium, in the fourth month, when the full moon is out, he will be at full strength'. We have a few months to prepare for his arrival," I said, walking away.

For the next couple of months, I looked around, books any transcripts we could find, looking for things that would lead me to Klaus and give me more knowledge of him. I had found a few small pieces of information but every time I found something it led to a dead-end.

I had yet another wall starting to be covered in information about this Klaus. I had one piece of information that intrigued me, he had been spotted with another person named Elijah. According to records Elijah played by his own rules, and would only help in matters when it suited him. However, the problem was that it was almost impossible to find him as apparently, he came to you, so there was nearly no hope.

I had done research into both of the men, there was only scraps. All the information on them was from people who had gone crazy. They were people in asylums. So none of it might be true, it could be all crazy guy stuff from all those people who went crazy. The only thing was Mrs Pearce wasn't crazy, she was one of ten people who fought this evil.

This thing was just one long roller coaster. I needed to talk to someone on the other side. But they would only come if they really truly in their hearts wanted help and if so they would come at will. I can't make them come against their own will. My powers didn't work that way.

The Legend

It had now been twelve weeks since we learned more about this devil man. Lately, I have been having flashes, they were painful, ringing, most of all, grief. All I could feel was grief and pain. They were in my dreams, constantly giving me horrors. I didn't tell the guys as the visions were clear enough to tell what was going to happen.

Last night's dream was different though, most of my visions are depressing and painful but this one was the opposite or completely different. It was about two men; one was who dressed as if he was going to go to a fancy party in a proper suit and the other was dressed with a leather jacket, jeans, and a black t-shirt. Both men were said to be considered quite handsome.

There wasn't much of a detailed description of either of them there was no reference to specific facial features or which was which in terms of clothing. Both men were powerful, both wolves, however, one stronger than the other.

The legend goes:

Et iterum venit malus,

Et roborabitur fortitude eius reduceret,

An angel faciam eum ad illam cadere,

Et mittentis sagittam fugit ad trahendum telum, quod minuat potestas,

Est solitarius lupus ostendamnillius plenus potential,

Geminos unum non separari potest unum perit vitae,

sanguine suo corruet et trident eum,

quod mala et mirabilius vincerentur.

In English it means:

'The evil will come again,

His power will regain,

An angel will make him fall for her,

An archer will pull the arrow that will diminish his power,

A lone wolf will show his full potential,

Twins will be separated one lives, one dies,

His own blood will betray but will fall with him,

The evil will be vanquished'.

Many times, I had read over the legend over and over again. Courtney (Lux) came to visit, and she really wasn't any help, but she said the evil is real and not a force to be reckoned with.

Her words were, "The man you seek will find you and wolves will come at his command. He is stronger than you think. No mortal will unsee his methods of killing. If I were you, I would run. And don't look back. I will mourn for you when you die."

Her words were crystal clear and I understood why those who have witnessed him have gone crazy. 'No mortal will unsee his methods of killing', what she meant was that what you saw of his wrath will come back to haunt you in your dreams.

Many people only believe he is a myth and a legend but from what Courtney said he is no myth or legend he's the real devil or evil. I guess that anyone who tries to defeat him will die at his hand but they legend says he will finally fall but it's apparently impossible unless he has a sweet spot like a weakness, we would just have to find out what it was.

The more I read over the legend the more it started to relate to me and friends, but something wasn't clear. What did they mean by the twins being separated, were they talking about Jax and Jake or, would it mean that either Frankie or Mickie was going to die before we defeated this mad man. This must have been what the visions have been trying to tell me that the twins won't be together for much longer.

Two days later, the vision became clearer it showed me what was going to happen to the twins, although it didn't tell me whether it was Frankie or Mickie. I couldn't bring myself to tell either of them, I couldn't tell anyone. I had to hold out hope that there was a way to alter the course of the vision. The only thing I did tell them was about Elijah and Klaus.

Greetings

Today's date was the 18th of February 2000. The boys were out on patrol as there was a rumour about a group of robbers in a bank. Vinnie went down in his wolf form as he wanted to tag along. I stayed behind because I said I wasn't feeling well but in truth, I had a vision the other night where the current events were happening and that I was meeting the man in the suit, that was the reason why I stayed behind, so all my visions could come true.

While I was waiting for the man to turn up, I did more digging through the archives from the league as they seemed to know more about somethings compared to any history book. What I found was most confusing it said, '*angelus autem diaboli cadunt, sed in ea cadunt quae prius ei non cadunt in paucitate*'.

It meant 'the angel will fall for the devil, but he will fall for her first, she will fall for him at his weakest'.

What did it mean? In both pieces of text that intrigued they both said the angel for the devil/the great evil. The legend referred a lot to us lot, so if Vinnie was the lone wolf. The suit man was the devil's blood. An archer was Roy. Half of twins was either Frankie or Mickie. I was the angel.

I was reading through old league books for the fifth time when I smelled something fresh; grass, bleach, and polish. Someone new had entered the building my instincts were telling me to be on alert, he must be the man in the suit. How the hell did he get in here without setting off the alarm?

126

Lately we had put alarms around the place since Roy broke in, before he switched sides, in case anyone else came and sabotaged us, it was to prevent people finding out who we are, what we were and getting hold of the league books.

I kept my metal staffs close I grabbed both of them so that I had one in each hand. I slowly rose out of my seat walking around the base to see where the intruder was. His scent lead me to the centre of the base. I was behind one of the pillars surrounding the centre of the base.

"Come out come out wherever you are, if you think you can beat me, you are just as foolish as everyone else who has come in my path," he called out in a large booming voice.

He picked up my scent, his shoes clicking against the concrete floor as he walked towards the pillar I was hiding behind. "I know you're there, come out and maybe I'll spare your life."

I quickly shapeshift into Roy so that he didn't know who I was. I make sure that I have a knife in my hand that I cover with my sleeve, with the blade in my palm. I slowly walk out from behind the pillar, still holding the staffs in my hands I look up at his face, his face was very square shaped he had dark brown hair. His suit was light grey. The shirt was a pristine white shirt, his tie was perfectly tied.

"Drop your weapons," he said in an annoyed tone. "Reveal your true face, I know you are not that person."

My lips trembled but I shifted back into my original form I dropped my weapons keeping my hands in the air. I still kept my blade strapped to my wrist, didn't want to be completely unarmed He looked me up and down. I was trying to keep my breathing to a minimal. He walked up to me and slowly placed a hand on my face.

127

"You, you're the angel he falls for, not surprising, your beauty is quite remarkable."

I kept my mouth shut tight my breathing became loud as I breathed heavily through my nose.

I moved the small blade down from my wrist to my hand so that the butt of the knife was in my hand. I tried to stab him in the side, but he stops my hand. His grip on my hand was like a weightlifter it was bone-breaking. The knife drops onto to ground as I feel my hand breaking.

"Now, now I'm not here to hurt but rather help you, do tell me, where are the others? I thought I would have an audience waiting for me." His hand around my throat.

"They're out facing my enemy I stayed behind as I knew you were coming; thought you were the devil that we were going to face," I speak. My airways began to feel strained as his grip became slightly tighter with each passing minute.

He releases me from his grip. My hand shoots towards my throat while he walks around the base, his shoes clicking against the floor. I can't see anything when I look at the future. I can't tell whether anything bad happens or if he really is here to helps us. His face remains calm and blank. Showing no emotion. He looks back towards me. I try to stand my ground.

"You have no reason to fear me, Zari Marie Kingston. I'm Elijah," he says offering his hand out as if we were meeting for the first time and that nothing had happened just a few minutes ago.

I ignore his hand, looking at his face. "You got a last name or do you not trust me. But judging by the way you changed your demeanour from 'I'm going to attack you' to 'hey this is the first time we are meeting' I'd say you have little trust."

He merely smirked and laughed quietly. Putting his hands in

128

his pockets and continuing to stroll around the base like he owns the place. He finally stopped at the picture of my family.

"You have a beautiful family. You're just like your mother. Klaus had a thing for her too. But then again, he is a monster."

I was intrigued by his words. Nothing was clear. How the hell has this man been unknown to the world when he clearly played a massive part in everything. But there was no knowledge, no information, no nothing on him.

"How'd you know my mother? How come there's next to nothing about you or Klaus? You seem to know everything about me, how?" I ask in a demanding tone trying to stand my ground, but I was failing miserably.

"Me and Klaus have been around for a long time Dear Girl. Back when your mother and her friends tried to defeat Klaus, he thought she was the angel, but she only showed hate towards him. I like to be discreet whereas Klaus does not, so I clean up his mess to protect Klaus and myself. But that is something for another time. I know you as your mother knew you were the angel, she asked me to watch you and protect you from anything and do anything necessary to keep you safe."

Confusion

Even more questions swirled my mind. How did my mother know? Why did she want me protected? Who is Klaus to Elijah?

He told me more about Klaus how they had been roaming the earth for three hundred years; he said the two of them were trying to find a way to become mortal but a century ago Elijah and Klaus didn't see eye to eye. Klaus decided he wanted to stay the way they were. Klaus knew something was going to stop him, so he did research on the legend and anything that relates to his end in being an immortal. I thought maybe Klaus was more than just a friend to Elijah maybe a relative or something. He talked about how they travelled the world and discovered the wonders of the world.

Once he had finished telling me everything, he was willing to tell me on this visit before the boys came back. I told him to leave.

He told me, "If you ever need me say the word '*auxilium*' and I will be there in a second."

I nodded as he gently held my face. In the blink of an eye, he was gone. I let out a breath I didn't know I was holding.

By the time I snapped back into reality the boys had come back. I turned to face them with a smirk on face. They looked rough, bruises and blood all over them luckily none of them were really hurt just a couple of scrapes and maybe a broken nose. I ordered them to get cleaned up while I cleaned up all my books.

"How'd the mission go?" I asked.

"Well, we were wrong, it wasn't Ollie it was this older middle-aged guy, blond hair, leather jacket; he looked like a complete psycho. He kept trying to kill Frankie," Mickie said with concern at the end for his twin brother.

"From the intel my friends with Ollie gave us they said he was staying with the shadows for a bit, something to do with this psycho, but he asked, 'where is the angel' we had no idea what he meant," Roy said.

"It's him Zari he's come. He wants you," Vinnie says eyeing me. I looked away knowing what he meant. The others didn't understand what he said.

They shot me questioning glances. So, I went to find the board I had been using to put all my research on. They all looked shocked, they read the line that intrigued them the most, the one which talked about them. I was worried about Frankie and Mickie as they were going to lose each other one of them was going to die.

"You two knew that one of us is going to die. Do you know whether it's me or Mickie?" He looked at me and Vinnie, nothing but anger was on his face.

We both looked at each other then back at the three. I looked down and said, "There's no way of telling which one it is, we couldn't bring ourselves to tell you. We didn't know how."

They walked off leaving me and Vinnie looking at the ground. Roy looked up at us apologetically. We talked Roy through everything we had learnt and asked him if he could tell the twins.

I went up to my room where I felt something was off, I looked around and saw a note on my bed 'dear angel, meet me in the woods you know where'. I knew who it was. I wasn't too sure whether I should go or not. But I did, I went in my suit minus my mask. Prepare for the worst, hope for the best.

I was drawn to the woods, no doubt about it, that it was going to lead me to something bad was still to be determined. My werewolf side wanted to take control and lead me to the meeting place. When I had left the building, my wolf was screaming to take control. I let the wolf take control it was almost like I was the passenger they knew where to go. After a while of running, we finally stopped at a cliff near the very edge of Liverpool, the overview on the sea was truly magical combined with the sunset colours. I sensed something behind me I pulled out a baton from my belt and held it in my hand with a tight grip.

"Seems like you found me love, though can I not see the face of the one whom I am to fall for."

I take a deep breath closing my eyes while I slowly turn around. Once I have fully turned, I open my eyes to see a man with dirty-blond hair he looked around my height maybe a little taller he had a small muscular, figure he looked around the age of thirty but in truth he was probably 330. His facial features were enchanting he looked like the most handsome person I have ever seen.

"Well, Elijah did say your beauty was unreal," he says, slowly walking up to me gently placing a hand on my cheek. "You look like your mother."

"Why'd you ask me here?" I ask looking at his eyes.

"Well can't I meet someone in a formal way before you try to kill me. I've heard a lot about you, Zari Marie Kingston, even before you were born." He pauses for a moment, "You look a lot like her."

As I blink, he's gone but leaves me a note in my hand saying 'ut scis unde mihi'—'you know where to find me'. I look around to see if he went in any direction, but it was unknown. He just

132

seemed to vanish into thin air, neat trick.

I decided to walk back to the base, Klaus had left me with many questions. Who did I look like? Why did he want to meet? Why did he care about me? Was I more than just someone who was going to take him down in his eyes? Who am I to him?

Questions but no answers.

By the time I had gotten back to the base it was late night to early morning. The boys were sound asleep, I could hear their snoring due to my enhanced hearing. I smiled to myself. Shrugging off my jacket, I looked towards the board that was full of information that couldn't be contained.

The sun shone through at around six or seven. The guys came groggily down the stairs rubbing their eyes. I had bought a horn a few days ago and pushed the button down, the noise was excruciating but it was satisfactory; their faces were all I need to make me smile.

"Well good morning to you lot," I said in a jokey voice.

"You could have told us where you were going, we were up most of the night looking for you and we thought you were dead then you go blowing a horn being all jokey and acting as if nothing happened last night," Frankie screamed at me.

"You don't get it, do you? I want to tell you everything, but I can't they won't let me and every time there's a consequence and I can't tell you till the time was right. Last night I met up with Klaus, he told me things and you won't understand anything that I got told because I don't. I don't know why he asked me to meet him but I'm glad I did," I retorted at him.

Taking a deep breath, I said, "I'm going for a walk to the hospital to check on Charlie," and walked away.

I decided that walking like normal people was the best option and a way to blend in with everyone. It was different and nice to feel normal and like I'm like everyone else. It wasn't too far from the hospital, it was the same one I was in when a bomb went off at my childhood home.

I walked up to the front desk asking politely which room Charlie was in. 2113.

Walking down the pale walls was giving me headache seeing the doctors and nurses showed me that there were genuinely good people in the world which was always a beautiful sight. I smiled to each person I passed until I reached Charlie's room. The door was closed. I opened it slowly and peaked through to see Big Boy and Charlie play on a brand new PlayStation. Their eyes were basically glued to the screen.

The room was small by sum standards, but for a hospital room with one bed, I guess it was roomy and it even had a window.

"Looks like you've gotten better," I said breaking their train of thought. They twisted their heads around so quickly that their heads could have fallen off. I walked over to them giving them a big hug, laughing and just being normal.

"Well if isn't it the woman who found me on the floor." We laughed whilst I hugged him carefully, so I didn't give him more pain than he was in.

"I heard Lauren got out a couple of days ago, how long till you'll be out?" I asked.

"Should be in a few days but I am actually enjoying not going to work as all I get to do is sit around and play games with this guy." We all burst out into laughter.

We spent the next couple of hours just laughing and having fun. Eventually Big Boy had to leave to get back to the workshop.

"It wasn't Ollie was it." I turned to look at Charlie.

"It was someone else, he said his name was Klaus and that

he was looking for you. You're hiding something aren't you?" he says looking at me dead in the eyes.

"I guess the cat's out of the bag. All of it is true. Klaus is looking for me and yes, I am hiding stuff from you and I'm doing to keep you safe I-I didn't want you getting involved," I reply solemnly.

"Give him hell for me will you give him pay back," he says with that smirk which he couldn't pull off without us lot bursting into laughter.

I gave him one final hug before leaving his room with a smile. In the room I felt normal, like I was the version of myself before everything went the way it was but I wouldn't change it. However, things were about to get harder and more painful, a fight was coming and the small moment like when I was with Charlie made a difference in my life. I knew that my life was never going to be the same again, massive changes were taking place, reshaping life as I knew it.

Preparation for the next event was about to begin.

Two days we worked preparing for every eventuality. Nothing no disturbances or visits from either Elijah or Klaus. A few more days passed and then everything changed attacks from all directions that lasted two days. The past two days' recent attacks strike my home and my group. Many relating to my kind. Four dead. Ten injured. Proof of who was behind the attacks was difficult to find. Klaus was drawing me out. Looking for a way to get under my skin, that was my gut feeling. The boys had gone out for a small recon mission. Meanwhile I thought it was time for a little history lesson.

"Auxilium," I say aloud.

As if clockwork. A man stood before me.

"Good to see you again, Ms Kingston," Elijah spoke upon

his arrival. I smiled to myself.

I wanted to get to know about how Elijah and Klaus came to be the way they are and learn a few things about Klaus in general and why he is a mad man.

"Three centuries ago, me and Klaus were travelling on order from our father."

I thought to myself 'how can they be related?'

"We came to Europe on a quest for money. However, we stumbled across a witch of many talents, her name was Kateri. Both Klaus and I had our suspicions about her more me than Klaus. Over time he was allured by her beauty, but she had other plans, you see, she was immensely powerful, the timeless woman, she turned us into to similar beings like her. However, all creatures have a weakness, we tried kill ourselves thinking that we could be free broken from the curse. It didn't work, she left the legend and throughout time, me and Klaus have tried to break the curse although over the past years he has tried to prevent the breaking of the curse, not sure why he's changed his focus."

All this information was a lot to take in but somehow clear. How? Why did Klaus stop wanting to break the curse? We spent the next hour or two talking about their history what their life was like. Hearing the perspective of major events in history was fascinating, learning history from a person who has actually experienced these things.

"Elijah, can I ask question?" I ask out of the blue, after a history lesson.

"Go on," he replies in a deep voice.

"What did the witch look like?"

He was hesitant to reply.

After a few moments of thinking he said, "You."

136

I was confused. Me? How could the witch be me?

"You were the witch. Reincarnation is all true, you're a replica of her. The one thing you don't have in common is your heart. Yours is pure and kind whereas she was dark and empty." I heard a faint noise in the background. "I must leave I don't think your friends would be happy to find me here." He rose out of his chair, smiled and within a blink of an eye he was gone.

I stayed the way I was looking down in my book reading on about the evil, aka Klaus. What made Klaus known to be evil? What was his grudge against a few of the wolves? How did those families make him weak? How are we going to prevent or end what is going to happen?

The boys came back looking better compared to last time. I smiled at them, and they smiled back. They didn't have any blood on them which was a good sign although they did look rather shattered. They slowly walked up to their rooms and crashed. I could hear their snores, they were peaceful. I decided to take the risk to visit Klaus again.

I left a note on the side so that the boys knew that I went out so that they didn't have a go out looking for me again because of me not telling them where I was going. I ran in my wolf form to the cliff side, the place was perfect. Just like the place Vinnie had shown me, where your thoughts and worries wash away at the sight of pure calm and tranquillity.

I sense a presence behind me, but I acted as if I hadn't notice I shapeshifted into Frankie just to test something out, sitting there was just normal and perfect. Peace.

"Seems like the lambs come to the slaughter, finally come to meet your fate," he says in a devilish tone compared to the previous tone I had heard him say to me.

I slowly rise to my feet and turn around and face him. I

received a smirk from him and I smirk back shifting back to myself. His expression quickly changes from devil/evil to pure shock. He can barely speak. Mouth moving but no sound.

"You're trying to kill Frankie, aren't you? He's the twin who dies. Why? Answer me!" I yell at him. I could feel the blood pumping around my body.

"He dies as it will complete the spell to break mine and Elijah's curse. I'll explain why a twin must die. An archer will use an arrow that has an herb which will bind the mortality together. The lone wolf will trigger our wolf side and you will give away your power of seeing the dead," he speaks.

Give away the power? How am I supposed to give away my power? We stayed talking for a little while and he explained everything. The giving away of the power, the mortality anything I wanted to know.

"There is no other way, is there," I say after peaceful silence. He looks at me then looks down. "To break the curse without him dying."

"If there were any other way I wouldn't but I want my wolf form and mortality," he says looking off to the sunset. "When I first was immortal, I always wanted to keep it, however, I soon realised along with Elijah that nothing would last and we would be lonely." The heartbreak in his eyes was clear the past 300 years had been complicated for him and yet he still held his head high.

We continue to talk about our fate and how the ritual would work. My part was to give my ability of seeing the dead to them so that they could regain mortality and finally find peace.

By the time we had finished, the sun was about to break I hadn't noticed the time, or the sun go down.

"Well, my love I would love to stay, however I do believe that your friends will be waiting for you and that you will need to prepare them for what lies ahead of us," he said with guilt. He stood up looking towards the ocean and the skyline that lay before us.

"Thank you for the answers I have been searching for," I replied standing beside him.

We shared a glance and a smile. In a blink of an eye, he was gone, once more I found myself smiling. If I were to live forever, I could never imagine what I would do, I would probably end up like Klaus but how would I find peace? Where is all the peace in this madness?

I ran off in wolf transformation, it was peaceful. Feeling the wind through my hair. The smells filling my nose. The dirt beneath my paws. The birds chirping in my ear. All these senses and feelings were always a taste of home, a place of peace. If I could stay this way forever I would. Peace was real. Or was it just a piece of imagination.

When I arrived back at the base it was midday. I had been gone for many hours. Walking through the doors I could see that the boys were quietly sleeping on piles of books and pieces of paper. How I wished that they weren't brought into this life. Vinnie was brought in by blood. Roy was brought in by foe. The twins were brought in by friend.

Each one of us has a purpose in life to fulfil just some of us have to die or face the consequences in order to fulfil our purpose.

"Auxilium," I breathe out silently. "Elijah."

"Zari what do I owe the pleasure today," he responds behind me.

New Friends

I explained to Elijah the recent event from when we last talked to now including my encounters with Klaus and learning the fate of Frankie but also that of myself. He seemed astounded at the information I had learned. I informed him that we would tell the team that he was working with us and what the goal was in helping Klaus and himself.

"Look alive men," we called out, however, the boys were heavy sleepers. I loved watching them sleep as they looked at peace. I huffed as in our attempts they would just not wake up. "Oi! Up you scallywags! Look alive."

They jolt awake the minute I finish my sentence. They are alerted. Eyes darting across the room, they finally land on me and Elijah. They look at us with confusion. After over an hour of explaining everything to them from Elijah's story and Klaus to my powers and Frankie's death. They were confused yet they understood what they learned and how we could get Klaus to lose his power.

"So let me get this straight you're his brother who is also immortal, but one is a psychopath and the other one is a normie. You want us to help you become mortal as both of you want to find peace even though Klaus killed the original people who stopped him the first time around," Roy questioned.

"Do you wish for me to explain what you are getting confused about?" They all nodded at Elijah's words. "Basically, years ago, when Vinnie and Zari's parents appeared we thought

140

they were the ones from the legend, however, the test was to see if she had feelings for Klaus this was before we learned more about our curse and that we need Zari's power over the dead, when we learned that she wasn't the angel, they still put up a good fight and tried to defeat us however they only weaken us."

"How long have you waited for the day you become mortal again?" Frankie asked.

"Since the day I became immortal; I lost my family, and I couldn't join them. Klaus realised after Sarah died it wasn't Klaus who killed her but people who learned of the witch who cursed us, they wanted to make sure that we didn't become mortal again. The witch vowed that we would never find peace or happiness."

We continued to talk about fate and everything that needed to be done to help Klaus and Elijah become mortal once again. Eventually Klaus joined us, fear was plastered across the boys' faces.

"Don't tell me you started the party without me," Klaus smugly spoke.

"Behave yourself," Elijah told him.

We got Klaus' side of the story and how he saw everything and why he wanted the mortality. Once you got to know the man you would see that he wasn't a complete psychopath but a lost person. They were both lost and trying to find their way back to the road of life.

By the time we had finished it was nightfall. The boys had fallen asleep, I was half asleep but the thought of being asleep with Klaus in the room just frightened me, what with Klaus going to kill Frankie and Klaus' interest in me. Even though Elijah was there I was still frightened. Frankie had finally come to terms with him dying but the thing that upset him most was leaving

Mickie all alone. But Mickie was never going to be alone.

"Dear brother shall we leave our new friends to sleep, we need to prepare for what is ahead of us," Elijah speaks

"You go on head I need to talk to Zari." I perk up at my name.

Elijah is gone in a blink of an eye I look up and see Klaus lurking near me, looking at me with a genuine smile.

"I know you're not looking towards the future. Frankie's death, losing people, your abilities but just know that I will be there for you always. I'm not looking forward to killing Frankie as he is a good kid just trying to right some wrongs, but it will be a kind death." He smiles and right before my eyes he disappears. I can't help but thinking that Klaus is really not looking forward to taking Frankie's life, his whole demeanour suggests that it's the last thing he want's but an unfortunate necessity to achieving his mortality.

With that as my final thought, I fall asleep into a peaceful slumber.

Old Faces

The next morning was peaceful. I found everyone asleep except Frankie. My nose perked up I could smell fresh eggs, bacon, and sausages. I walked to the kitchen which was upstairs at the end of the corridor where you could get a beautiful view of the city. I quickly stopped by my room to freshen up after the past few days.

I silently creep up into the kitchen Frankie was happily humming away even with everything going on he was still able to find the good in things. He turned around with perfectly cooked sausages.

"I thought you were the twin who couldn't cook," I speak with a grin on my smile.

He giggles. "No, I'm the twin that can cook. Mickie, bless him, can't, but he is the twin who can make refreshing cocktails." He smiles.

We plate up the meals ready for the others to wake up they were slowly waking up. I laid the table out we never normally do this because we never have the time but today it just feels important almost special that we take the time and savour the moment. The food was spectacular I hadn't had a proper breakfast since the day I left my family which was three years ago.

We finished breakfast and I told the boys that I would go on the patrol seeing as I had been avoiding going out to learn more about Klaus and Elijah. But its best if I could see if anyone needed my help or if Bretherstone had made any recent appearance as lately with the arrival of Klaus he has been off-

143

grid which worried me. Who knows what he could be plotting?

The best way to see the entire city was at the clocktower where Vinnie took me. A few moments pass with me going from roof to roof with no activity when I smell a scent which I don't want to. Bretherstone.

I follow the scent; the path I follow feels familiar. I follow the scent until it leads me to the house, I hoped I would never return to the house which caused all of this. The problems and everything else that has happened over the past three years. However, it seemed to be more run-down than the last time.

"Well, well it's been a while," Bretherstone says being his usual self.

What did he want? "I thought you had died seeing as you disappeared as quick as lightning when my friend appeared," I replied.

"I disappeared as I got threatened by a complete psycho. He said that if I interfered in his plan, he would kill me and bury me twelve-foot underground. Plus, if I ever so much as hurt you in any way I was told to run for the rest of my life." He breathes out walking around me.

He continues to circle me. "If this is some sort of game it isn't any good. Why are you back if Klaus doesn't want you around why did you come back?"

"Simple. I got bored," he responded standing in front of me pulling a devil's smirk.

He lunges at me with a fist aiming at my face, I dodge him, however, he hasn't been lounging around whilst I've been dealing with Klaus. He's become stronger. We fight with our bodies. He whistles. I become surrounded.

"You really believe that I would come alone when I know that you would find me," Bretherstone says walking towards his minions.

Slightly worried I whisper, "Auxilium." I pray that he heard me or at least someone did so that they could bring me help but no luck they didn't arrive.

I was outnumbered. Hope was gone how was I supposed to defeat twenty odd men all on my own with no weapons. They were sent out in fives. Starting strong was a good tactic for the first two rounds. When it came to the third round, I was losing strength and the will to keep going. I was prone to punches rather than dodging them.

I was on the floor blood dripping from my mouth, suddenly I was yanked up as one of the men placed me in a headlock. He pulled me to my knees. I was struggling against his grip. My eyes started to feel heavy as my vision closed in. Suddenly, the feeling of being choked and the pain in my arms disappeared. A strange sensation came over me I felt safe in that moment, nothing was hurting me. I catch my breath and regain my vision.

I turned around to see all of them there with each fighting one of the men that was against us. However, I couldn't see Klaus or Bretherstone. I get up from the floor to see most of our enemies on the floor. The boys continued.

"Are you all right?" Elijah asks, walking up to me. I silently nod.

We hear grunts coming from the other room. We look at each other and run towards the noise. We see Klaus and Frankie fighting Bretherstone. They throw good punches at each other. They seemed to be putting up a good fight. I see a blade reflect on the light from the lightbulbs.

I intervene trying to pry the blade out of Bretherstone's hands, but he was too strong for me and I was struggling against his grip, my hands were still on his hands to try and stop him from stabbing me in the chest. Frankie pulled Bretherstone away from me while he was distracted.

"You won't hurt my friend," Frankie says.

"Then I'll hurt you," he retorted. He stabbed Frankie in the gut turning around wrenching it up slicing through him. We all stared in pure, utter shock. Mickie looked like a part of his soul was just ripped out of him. Blood was pouring out of Frankie's mouth.

"Guess your chess move didn't work," Bretherstone says emotionless.

We were all in our own dimension trying to figure out what was going. When we snapped back into reality Frankie was on the ground, we all moved so that we could try to help him. His pulse was weak. His breath was hoarse and uneven.

"Stay with us, okay, we're going to get you home and safe," Mickie says, tears flooding down his face.

"See to my fate," Frankie directs at Klaus. He nods shedding a silent tear.

He looks at me and Elijah knowing full well what Frankie wanted. He wanted peace. We were told to take the others away so that we didn't have to witness Frankie's death. Especially not Mickie. We stand up and take Mickie, Roy, and Vinnie away so they wouldn't have the memory plastered in their brains for the rest of their lives. Roy and Vinnie went quietly and without too much fuss. However, it took all of Elijah's strength to pull Mickie away from his twin. The distraught look on his face was heart-breaking.

We took them away, all of us were struggling against Mickie to try to get him away. However, in our best attempts we couldn't get him away, so we did the most humane thing possible. Knock him out. We placed him in his room when we got back to base. We sat down in silence not sure how to take the last day.

The Curse

We couldn't move, speak, or even look at each other. Eventually after what felt like an eternity Klaus came back with Frankie wrapped in cloth, we could see that Klaus took care with Frankie's body. I looked back and saw Mickie's door was still closed. We weren't sure how he would take the pain of losing his twin.

Klaus laid him on the table gently, reaching into his pocket he pulled out two vials of blood.

"I take it that you not only had to kill Frankie but drink his blood." Vinnie says looking at Klaus. He nods. "What part do I play as I know 'a lone wolf will show his full potential' so what do I do."

"You will give us the gift you possess, you will bite, which will essentially restore our wolf side completely. We still have speed and strength, but our wolf form needs to be restored and a bite will do the trick," Elijah says in his natural tone.

"Shall we get this charade over and done with so we can put Frankie to rest properly." I stand up emotionless, looking at all of them. "Let's get this over and done with."

They all nod.

"Stand in a circle around me and Klaus. Then we will take it in turn on who does what we will call you forward and tell you what to do," Elijah responds, pointing us each to a spot.

We are all in position. First up was Roy, he had to stab both of them in the shoulder with the special arrow we found it in

Klaus' possessions the arrow was special as it somehow had a link to the witch. He first stabs Klaus, muttering something to Klaus that was inaudible. Roy says nothing to Elijah and plays his part. When he came back to his spot, he seemed to be the same but better guess he said something that needed to be said.

Then it was Vinnie's turn. Vinnie looked for guidance from Elijah and Klaus, however they didn't respond but simply stayed still. It was almost like they were saying you know what to do. He bit both Elijah and Klaus next to their wounds from where Roy stabbed them. When he came back to his respective spot something was different about him. I remember my father saying that when you bite someone, they become a part of your pack unless they leave you. Vinnie had become an alpha.

The next part was drinking Frankie's blood. Their movements were in sync. They downed the blood easily as if it was water, however, the scrunch of their noses signified that the taste of blood was revolting.

I wasn't sure on how exactly I was supposed to relinquish my power, but I knew it was a vital part of the curse. I step forward feeling a gush of air pass me. Closing my eyes. Then reopening them I see that the scenery is different. Looking around. My double, Kateri, she was the spitting image of me. The only difference was our clothes.

"Seems like the noblemen have found their freedom which they don't deserve," she says in a monotone. "Repeat after me, *'mortalitas ista donum est donum, et ego vobis'.*"

"*Mortalitas ista donum est donum, et ego vobis,*" I repeat.

"*I, ait, ista malediction liberabo te.*"

"*I, ait, ista malediction liberabo te,*" I repeat.

My eyes close and open again. I find myself back at the base. Klaus and Elijah are on the floor along with the others. I check each of their pulses luckily, they were fine. Elijah and Klaus had one before all of this only time would tell if it worked and was worth the sacrifice.

I wait around on one of the boxes thinking that I'll never be able to see Jake any more until I die. I enjoyed the conversations we used to have but I won't be able to have them till I die. I guess my gift was a privilege then I gave it away to save others and it will be worth it.

They grunt. Slowly getting up, wincing, looking around.

"What in the world happened how are you not like the rest of us," Roy asks looking at the others whilst they get up as well.

"I have no idea but before we can all go back to the way things were and stop Bretherstone we have one thing left to do and all of us are going," I respond.

Passing to the Next Life

For the past few days, we planned the funeral for Frankie. Currently I was the only one at the casket ready for the funeral to begin. Not even the priest was here just me and the casket.

I go up to Frankie the head door was still open so that we could say goodbye before we put him to rest all of us who had fallen were buried on a plot of land or mementos. My family had mementos whereas Frankie was going to be actually buried here.

I had inherited the land after my mother had died. So, I decided to turn it to a private graveyard for my family and Frankie was my family. The land was only a couple of acres only a small plot of land. The scenery was magical, surrounded by willows the gravestones shaded by the leaves. Lilies and orchids highlighted the pathway.

I walk up to the spot where Frankie would be laid to rest. "Is it bad luck to talk to the soul who has passed before he has been properly laid to rest. I hope you find peace *ave atque vale*," I say with a saddened smile.

Standing there looking at his face I sensed a presence behind me. Turning round I saw that it was Klaus the great evil was bottled up with remorse and heavy emotions.

"Klaus it's not your fault, whatever Roy said it's not true," I tell him, placing my hands on his face.

"That's not the point, Roy asked was it a mercy or pity and it was a kill to stop all the pain and help him find peace; I stabbed him through the heart, Zari. Did I do it for me or for him?" he responds spilling his emotions and thoughts

"You did it for both of you. Frankie knew that but he did know that you helped him find peace either way, someone was going to die everyone has their time, but you aren't a bad person."

He just looks down.

Moments of silence pass and the others all arrive. We all stood around and passed each other small glances. Eventually the priest arrived. Tommy was there, we told him the truth about his brother being killed, however, we didn't tell him about the ritual and that Frankie was working alongside me to defeat Bretherstone.

"Today we are gathered to celebrate the life of Frankie Jakes, a boy whose life was cut short," the priest continued with the prayers and everything he was supposed to do. We all said words about Frankie even Klaus and Elijah said words about Frankie. Frankie was always helping out making sure we took care of each other.

At the reception I was quietly having a drink, most of us had gone back to the base to rest. It was only me, Klaus, and Mickie left. The boys were talking while I was looking out the window. I listened in on their conversation.

"I forgive you but that doesn't mean that you have my complete trust."

"I know what it's like to lose family, after all, I have lived for a little over three hundred years."

I smile as they were patching up holes that needed repairing. I have a sip of my drink although after finishing my glass I see the last person I wanted to see. Bretherstone.

Walking out, I see he is watching my every move.

"Beautiful funeral."

"You weren't invited what do you want?" I retorted in a

151

demanding tone.

"I want the book," he responded.

"Well, you're not having it, you'll only use it for what you want and the purpose of it is to stop evil like you." I glared at him.

"See you at the next event," he said walking away with a smirk on his face.

"Can't wait."

Just when the thought of having a normal life was within reach, Bretherstone reared his evil head, just to remind us that this was going to continue.